She clutched her shaking hands in her lap, no longer able to look into Clara's eyes. Her voice trembled slightly as she quietly said, "I'd like to ask you something, Clara. And if you say no, I'd like you to promise you'll never tell what I asked."

Clara continued that easy smile. "All right. I promise."

Tessie unlocked her hands and moved the lantern to the floor, plunging them into soft shadows. "Would you mind ..." She cleared her throat, stalling. Ask her! her mind screamed. "Would you mind if I ... kissed you?"

GRASSY FLATS

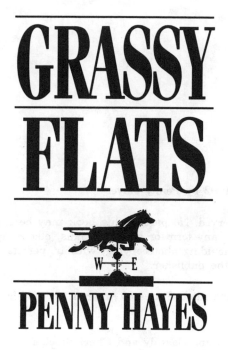

PENNY HAYES

The Naiad Press, Inc.
1992

Printed in the United States of America on acid-free paper
First Edition

Edited by Christine Cassidy and Cheri Stocker
Cover design by Pat Tong and Bonnie Liss
    (Phoenix Graphics)
Typeset by Sandi Stancil

Library of Congress Cataloging-in-Publication Data

Hayes, Penny, 1940–
    Grassy flats / Penny Hayes.
        p.   cm.
    ISBN 1-56280-010-8
    I. Title.
PS3558.A835G7   1992
813'.54--dc20
                                                              91-36896
                                                                   CIP

To Karen

And to my mother, Helen,
who remembered these times well

About the Author

Penny Hayes was born in Johnson City, New York on February 10, 1940. As a child she lived on a farm near Binghamton, New York. She later went to school in Utica and Buffalo, graduating with degrees in art and special education. She has made her living teaching most of her adult life in both West Virginia and New York State.

A resident of Ithaca, NY she lives with her lover of eleven years. Her interests include backpacking, mountain climbing, canoeing, traveling, reading, and early American history. She has been published in *I Know You Know*, *OF THE SUMMITS ò OF THE FORESTS* and various backpacking magazines. *GRASSY FLATS* is her fourth novel and she is hard at work on her fifth.

Books by Penny Hayes

The Long Trail	1986
Yellowthroat	1988
Montana Feathers	1991
Grassy Flats	1992

CHAPTER ONE

Frigid winds blowing off Lake Michigan pushed
and pulled at Clara Striker as she made her way
along Dayton Street. Loose strands of once-shining
blonde hair whipped around her face from beneath a
tattered, dirty woolen headscarf, its color no longer
distinguishable. With numb fingers she tied the scarf
tighter at her throat and pulled her ragged coat
snug against her thin body. Tucking her hands
beneath her armpits, she cursed the March weather
and bent into the vicious gales impeding her forward

momentum. She dreaded the prospect of spending the night alone on some unfamiliar Chicago street, not to mention having to face the killing weather.

Envying her husband, she glanced back toward the police station where she had just left him. Arrested for theft not an hour ago, Hank had been hauled off in handcuffs. The station, only a half a block away from the scene of the crime, was close enough so that the cops had allowed Clara to stay with him until he had been booked. She'd clung to his arm every step of the way.

It was *stupid* of Hank to have snatched those apples off that fruit stand. Yet she could hardly blame him. He had been complaining all afternoon about how hungry he was, and they didn't have a dime between them. For years, people by the thousands had been dying of starvation with government officials denying every year that anybody was. But Clara sure knew better and had watched more than one person pass on just that way.

Living in Bend, Oregon, she hadn't at first been affected by the Depression occurring three thousand miles away. Only with mild interest had she read of the country's troubles. Later, news reaching Bend had become more detailed and chilling.

A number of rich folks' entire lifes' savings had been wiped out on October 24, 1929. Black Thursday, the newspapers called it. When Clara heard of it, she envisioned people all over New York City dressed up in fancy ballroom dresses and black tuxedos standing around inverted glass bowls and watching yards of ticker tape devour their fortunes inches at a time. Some of the men committed suicide, she'd read. She also read that some women had killed themselves. *Women!* At that time, Clara couldn't even imagine a woman committing suicide. Now she could — easily.

Closer to her own pocketbook were the banks that she and millions of others throughout the country had trustingly put their money in. "Safe as a bank," her pa used to say about people and things he believed in. That was a laugh. With little or no advance warning, banks by the scores had closed, giving no hope that anybody could withdraw their savings. Clara had become one of those caught in the country's downfall.

Not long after, things really began going to hell. Bread dropped to three and a half cents a loaf, and few could afford that much. While thousands of bushels of apples rotted in Oregon orchards, kids ended up with rickets even as teachers gave up part of their salaries to help feed the children. Men slit the throats of entire flocks of sheep and threw them into canyons rather than have the animals starve to death because their shepherds couldn't afford to feed them and couldn't afford to ship them to market. People from the city moved to the country expecting it might be better there, and people from the country moved into the city thinking the same thing, and both groups were wrong.

All kinds of folks were thrown out onto the streets because they'd lost their jobs and couldn't pay their rents or mortgages. Clara had met dozens of them: plumbers, shoemakers, salesmen, newspaper printers, carpenters, school teachers, electricians, painters. There was even an aviator. But the one she was most grateful to meet during her travels was the dentist who was as threadbare as she. He had pulled three of her back teeth for free as she, Hank and the jawsmith rode east in a Union Pacific boxcar. All she had to give him was her plate of beans. She couldn't eat anyway after that workout and had gratefully passed them to him.

She squinted into the cold winds as she hastened past dozens of people huddling in doorways and alleyways. There were 10,000,000 people out of work this year. Mr. Roosevelt had said so on a radio broadcast she'd overheard in a store just last week. Right now it looked like half of those folks were wandering the streets of Chicago just as she was. Again, fear galloped through her as a blast of icy breezes slammed into her chest. She sank further into her coat and continued walking.

"Damn you, Hank Striker," she muttered, her teeth chattering, her lips stiff as she spoke. "Getting us in such a fix."

Ten years ago when she had been working in a roadside diner in Bend, Clara Striker had been a pretty woman. At eighteen, she had been happy. She once had long golden hair, flashing blue eyes and beautiful even teeth. A little plump, she hadn't ever minded. The boys seemed to enjoy that in her. Drivers coming through Bend, their logging trucks loaded with timber from the Three Sisters Mountains, stopped at the diner. Clara served them coffee and sandwiches and the best apple pie in Deschutes County.

Now she was thin; her eyes had lost their glow; her remaining teeth were rotting. Her hair had turned mouse-colored and was oily from lack of washing. She wore it loose, carelessly combing it once every few days, too tired to do much else. Her threadbare dress made from printed cotton feedsacks was the only one she owned.

Clara had married Hank six months after meeting him, and a year later, in 1930, his logging company shut down. Too proud to live on her salary, he had made her quit to go east with him so that he could find "something." They'd been all over the country a half dozen times since then.

After booking Hank at the station, the police made her leave the precinct. "But where will I go?" she'd pleaded. She could have slept in the truck tonight, but the thought that she might be molested kept her away.

"Women's Relief Home. Two blocks south on Oak Street," an officer had told her. "Free lodging. Pick up your old man in the morning." A strong arm had steered her toward the door, and that was that.

She was now walking the two blocks, fighting the shifting blow every step of the way. Upon reaching the imposing gray stone structure, she mounted the steps. With a stiff finger, she rang the bell.

Almost immediately, a wizened old woman answered the door. "Yes?"

"I've come to spend the night," Clara whispered. Her voice was nearly gone with the cold.

"Oh, I'm so very sorry, my dear," the woman answered. Her eyes looked sad, and her voice broke as she said, "There isn't a place left to put you. There're fifty beds here, and every one is already filled for the night. If you come back tomorrow morning around five, I could give you a spot to sleep in. The women start stirring about then."

5

"I could sleep on the floor," Clara suggested. "I wouldn't mind."

The woman sadly shook her head. "It's already promised. Every square inch. And all the chairs, couches and tables are filled. I'm sorry my dear."

"But what else can I do?" Clara asked, tears flooding her eyes. "Where can I go?"

"I suggest Grant Park, dear," the woman replied, patting Clara's cold hand. "Stay away from Lincoln Park. Women are having trouble over there. Good luck to you."

"Trouble?" For the second time this afternoon, a door closed in her face, and she was alone.

She started down the steps, looking first in one direction, then the other, muttering, "Grant Park, Grant Park. I got as much idea where Grant Park is as where Timbuktu is." Brushing freezing tears from her face, she asked herself, "How can it be so awful cold in March?"

She hated Chicago. Its streets were filled with the homeless: tramps, waifs, women of the night and peddlers selling pure junk, shouting at her as she passed them by. Who in the world needed a rubber ball these days, or a necktie? Newsboys hawked their papers, and nobody had a nickel to buy one.

She warmed herself several different times by stepping inside stores to thaw her hands and cheeks. She asked a stranger or two for directions, eventually arriving at Grant Park. She stood before it surveying the place. It was a large open space dotted with occasional trees and shrubs. In the dying light, women were gathering together — not just a few women, but dozens. Some had children with them; most seemed to be alone. All were in rags as bad as or worse than Clara's. Many were in men's trousers.

Clara wandered onto the grounds. At a distance, she watched a woman set up a large cardboard box and crawl inside. Curled up into a tight little ball, she pulled down the flap.

Clara moved off. There were oil barrels placed here and there throughout the park. People huddled around the drums, briskly rubbing their hands, warming them over the fire. Once in a while, someone threw in wood scraps or wads of paper. Clara caught a whiff of something cooking off to her left and went toward it.

"Get lost, honey," a big, dark-eyed woman warned as Clara drew closer.

Like an animal driven off, Clara scampered away.

She thought there must be a hundred women here now and more continually filtering in. Some made their beds on benches, others directly on the ground beneath leafless bushes; still others, like the first woman Clara had seen, huddled in boxes. Most, like herself, walked aimlessly about, looking for a spot to spend the night. She had no idea how she would survive without shelter. At least she had always had Hank's arms in cold weather — until tonight.

She was run off from two barrels and four cooking areas before a woman leaning against a tree called out in a rasping voice, "Come here, girl. I got no one to share with and nothing to share. You can sit with me."

Gratefully, Clara sank down beside the heavyset woman and tried to tuck her bare legs beneath her coat. The cold ground was painful to the touch.

"Come here, get closer. We can get warmer this way." The woman drew Clara against her, wrapping her arms around her.

The woman had a pungent smell. Her eyes were dull, her skin ashen; the flesh of her face was drawn tight over high cheekbones in spite of her bulk. She was gripped by a spasm of coughing, but throughout the spell, she never once let go of Clara. Finally she asked, "You got any food? Bread, fruit, anything?"

"No, nothing," Clara whispered, feeling guilty that she had nothing to offer the stranger whose size alone gave Clara the warmth she'd longed for all day as she had wandered from place to place with Hank while he looked for work. "I'm sorry," she added.

"Don't be," the woman said. "My name's Jenny. What's yours."

She shifted her weight, and Clara felt herself sink even deeper into the woman's flesh. "I'm called Clara," she answered.

"Been in town long?"

"A couple of days."

"This is a better park to sleep in," Jenny said. "Safer than over at Lincoln. Women have been getting grabbed over there."

Clara shuddered. "I'm only here for the night. My husband's looking for a job. No luck yet, though."

"Where is he?" Jenny asked, craning to look around. "Seems as though you'd be with him."

Clara didn't dare tell Jenny the truth. "He thinks he might find something at the railroad yards. He sent me here for the night while he stands in line.

It wouldn't do to have him saddled with a woman hanging around while he fights the line tomorrow."

"I wish your man luck," Jenny said. She closed her eyes, rested her head against Clara, and fell asleep instantly.

Hunger did that to people. No food — no reason to stay awake. Clara pulled her legs tighter against her body. Soon her breathing blended in with Jenny's.

In the gray dawn, Clara woke stiff in her bones. Over the years, she had slept on open ground, beneath countless bridges, in barns, in corn cribs, on hay mounds and in the truck. In the early days, she and Hank had often ridden boxcars and slept the miles away. Always, she woke stiff and sore. Last night she had dreamed of falling asleep and waking in a bed of her own. She'd had that dream a lot in the years she and Hank had been wandering from one town to another with their piss-poor jobs and piddlin' little pay.

She eased herself out of the arms of her sleeping benefactor. Once out of her grasp, Jenny's arms should have dropped, but they remained where they were, extended in a circular position as though they still held Clara.

Clara touched the woman's face. "Jenny?" She pushed at Jenny's arms which did not move. Jenny was dead.

Clara quickly glanced around. A few people

stirred; some were squatting behind bushes, others, firing up oil drums or cooking over low flames. But no one looked her way. Her heart thudding, she pushed Jenny's arms to her lap so that she looked as though she were sleeping.

Forcing the ghoulish behavior from her mind, Clara quickly searched Jenny's pockets. There were several letters which Clara left untouched and a locket without pictures which she also left alone. She fingered the hem of Jenny's dress. Just as she'd figured! She easily ripped the rotting thread, freeing the hem. Several coins and bills fell into her hand. She jammed the money into her pocket and again glanced around. Still no one paid attention to her.

She straightened Jenny's dress around her knees and pulled her coat tighter around her body and her hat lower over her face. It wasn't much kindness toward a woman who had given Clara the last of her warmth and all of her money, but it would have to do.

"Thank you for everything, Jenny," she whispered tearfully, gratefully. She squeezed the dead woman's hand and left the park.

Clara estimated it to be five-thirty. Already, the streets were jammed with horses and carts and the occasional car. Men loudly hawked puckered fruits and vegetables that had been stored in fruit cellars and sold a few at a time throughout the winter. The produce was protected from this morning's bitter cold beneath layers of hay and straw. She watched a young boy dart from an alleyway and steal an armload of potatoes before running off. A loud "Hey!" from the vendor didn't slow him down. The man was smart enough not to give chase. He'd lose the whole load to scamps if he did.

She hurried past the bustle and at six entered the precinct door. She waited on a hard bench against the back wall of the depressing-looking office while a sleepy-eyed officer fetched Hank. Hank's truck keys were returned to him with a stern warning from the sergeant. "We don't like vagrants here, mister. Don't get caught again. We know you did it just to get a bed and a meal. It won't go so good with you next time. You'd best get out of town."

"Let's go, Clara," Hank said gruffly. Over a grubby blue shirt and bib overalls much too large for him, he buttoned his long, black coat worn through at the elbows and in tatters at the hem. The collar was completely missing. His shoes were held together with twine. He kept his feet warm by stuffing newspaper in the soles. He donned a dark knit cap over his thinning hair and rubbed the stubble of his chin. "Sure wish I had a nickel. I need a cup'a coffee bad."

Outside, he pulled out the stub of a cigar and without lighting it, rammed it between his yellowed teeth. He was once a handsome man, well muscled and always smiling. Now he was gaunt. His deepset eyes smoldered with anger, and he always needed a shave.

"How'd you sleep?" Clara asked, hurrying through the door after him. She thought of the cot he'd probably had — and the blankets he'd slept beneath.

"They keep the place damn cold," Hank complained. "No heat at all."

"Did they feed you?" She wanted to know about the food, every bit of information he could give her, every scrap he'd eaten.

"If you call potatoes and ham 'food.' Stinkin' little piece'a ham. Swallowed it in one bite. You make out okay?"

"Yeah," she answered. She waited for him to ask how she had made out, but he didn't.

"Wish we had some dough," he said.

She fished out Jenny's money and passed it to him.

Eyeing her suspiciously, he asked, "Where'd you get this?"

"Found it on the street by a newsboy. Guess he got careless with it."

The answer seemed to satisfy him. Greedily, he counted it. "Four dollars and thirty-nine cents. Food and gas comin' up." Without thanking her, he jammed the bills and coins into his pants pocket and began walking so fast Clara nearly had to run to keep up with him. They headed for a small diner at the end of the street. There, they lingered over coffee and doughnuts, soaking up the warmth of the hashhouse's interior.

Eventually, the disheveled owner wiped his palms against a greasy apron and called to them from behind the counter. "You folks are done. You gotta get moving. I got customers needs those seats."

Clara looked around at the nearly empty establishment. The proprietor just didn't want to waste heat on riff-raff like them. She sighed as she rose.

"We're done in this town, anyway," Hank said.

"We'll get gas and head west. Might be warmer there by now. Let's hit a bread line first."

Clara was glad they'd be moving again, that they *could* move. Hank's one stroke of good luck in the last couple of years was his winning that old beat up '27 Ford pickup in a poker game. He'd cheated — but he'd gotten away with it.

Riding in the truck was far better than hitchhiking or riding in dangerous, drafty boxcars. Over the years she'd seen a number of men and boys killed beneath trains' wheels. They had died horrible, bloody deaths as they made futile attempts to board boxcars traveling at unsafe speeds. The trains had just kept rolling, and Clara and Hank kept rolling with them. The engineers never seemed to realize that anyone could lose a life beneath the tons of steel. That knowledge was left to the riders who watched helplessly from the open doors of the cars and who later said nothing to the railroad officials at the risk of being run out of the yards at the ends of clubs and threatened with guns for trespassing on railroad property.

And now she and Hank would be traveling west again. "You're not thinking of going back to Washington are you?" she asked.

"West, I said. Not northwest. Maybe California." Reaching the Ford parked along a side street, he pulled open the cab door and climbed in. "Let's go."

Clara was glad to oblige. "West," she repeated, settling herself inside.

"That's right," he answered.

As Hank maneuvered the truck down the street Clara closed her eyes, remembering the awful shame of learning that Hank, along with several other men, had deliberately set fire to one of Washington's forests just to create jobs as firefighters. Times had been tough. But she'd always doubted they'd been that tough.

Once she'd asked him to apply for relief. "Like hell!" he'd bellowed. "Stand in line all day long on the damn Court House steps. And then —" His face turned purple with rage — "to have some referee pick apart my life, like I ain't tried to get work. The judge sittin' up there lookin' at me like I was the one caused the stinkin' Depression and didn't deserve a nickel. Well, they can keep their nickel *and* their Depression. I didn't do it!" She didn't ask him again.

They'd been in that town a month. She couldn't remember its name anymore. Hank had gotten a job as a billboard poster. But then the men had struck, and Hank struck with them. Scabs took over, and that was the end of the only job he'd had for longer than a month in five years.

Soon after that, they'd moved on again. Hank tried everything that came along: washing dishes, cooking, running a gas station for a fellow, being a salesman and once, a shoemaker. She chuckled. Hank had quit on the spot when he'd smashed his thumb with a hammer. But it wasn't funny later when the repossessing company took away the couch they'd bought on time with his first paycheck.

Before leaving Chicago, they stopped at a bread line at a small church. Outside in a cold drizzle, they waited for an hour before each received a small bowl of soup, a watery paste of potatoes and salt and pepper. "Bread," Hank demanded.

"None today," said the pale-faced youth who

served them. He looked as hungry as Clara felt. "Red Cross didn't come."

An ugly look spilled across Hank's face. Clara quickly pushed him into the church. They settled down in a rear pew to eat. "We finish here, we're getting out," he vowed.

Clara nodded, thinking this the best soup she had ever tasted.

So used to humanity's hunger, she easily ignored the poverty surrounding her, the mass of men sucking noisily at their bowls, not bothering with spoons, wiping their mouths on soiled, threadbare coats. Their hair was long and dirty beneath woolen caps or old straw hats. Toes protruded through their shoes. Socks were a rarity. Whining children clung to mothers whose eyes flitted about and whose skin was sallow and translucent. The women carefully spooned the warm liquid into the pinched faces of their young, their eyes hollow, their cheeks sunken.

Finished in no time, Clara and Hank returned to the truck. After gassing up, they headed for the open highway, the city eventually giving way to spacious fields. Clara hoped Hank never wanted to return to Chicago, or to any other big town.

She closed her eyes, despair settling around her like a dark cloud. Dear God, she silently prayed. I'm cold, I'm hungry. And worse . . . Even silently, she couldn't say it. She opened her eyes to scan the countryside.

She was dozing off when she was jolted back to full consciousness by Hank's loud voice. "Get out of the way, you fools." He leaned on the horn. A family of four, the husband, his wife and their two little boys, were hitchhiking, standing in the middle of the road in a desperate attempt to get Hank to stop. "I got troubles enough without picking up tramps," he snarled. He clutched the steering wheel tighter and whizzed around them.

Clara kept her mouth shut. Not long ago, she and Hank had been tramps. But she didn't remind him, knowing she couldn't help the family they had just passed.

God save her, she could barely help herself.

CHAPTER TWO

"Uhhhh!" Aggie felt as if her heart soared out of her chest, bounced off the walls of the room, traveled through the opened window, and reached the stars before returning to earth to slam headlong back into her body. She gasped, arched her back, and collapsed in a spent heap. When she was able to move again, she snuggled tightly against Nell and whispered hoarsely, "You are the greatest living thing on earth." She could still feel searing heat racing up and down her inner thighs like hot branding irons being swiftly dragged along her flesh.

"As compared to what?" Nell asked. She knew what Aggie would say, and Aggie did.

"The sun rising, a flower blooming, a butterfly's wing, the ocean's ..."

"Shhh ..." Nell soothed Aggie's sweating brow. "Save your breath. You haven't said anything new in the fifteen years I've known you."

"Would you want me to?" Aggie asked.

"It would scare the hell out of me if you did." Nell pulled her closer. "Make me think you weren't paying attention."

"Never have I not paid attention to you in bed."

"Nor anywhere else that I can think of," Nell replied affectionately.

Aggie sighed contentedly. "We're pretty lucky, aren't we?"

Nell fitted herself against Aggie's familiar frame, lifting her own heavy breasts into a more comfortable position. "We're lucky — at least this way. But life ain't perfect, as they say."

"Who is they?"

"Try the bank. On second thought, forget the bank." Nell shook her head to tear the image loose. "Bad time to be thinking about it."

Aggie agreed. "It's —" By the light of a full moon, she read the bedside clock — "eleven o'clock. No one can get us now. That's the blessed relief of the middle of the night. Even the banker is in bed at this hour."

"Then we're safe for the moment," Nell replied.

Aggie rested her body over Nell's.

* * * * *

18

Dawn rose gray and warm. Nell stood on the back porch looking east. A dozen chickens pecked the ground around the porch. The milk cow lowed in the barn, impatient to be milked. It was unusually hot for late May. Nell hoped it was not an indicator of worse to come.

She strolled into the kitchen and sat on a spindle-backed chair at the gingham-covered table. With her elbow, she shoved aside a stack of bills as Aggie placed a plate of bacon and eggs in front of her. "We have to pay the feed bill," Nell said. "The rest can wait." She picked up her fork and with its edge, cut a slice of bacon in half and began to eat.

Aggie joined her and forked a piece of egg while shuffling through the stack until she found the bill. "Do we dare let the petrol account go any longer?"

"Have to," Nell replied. "And Rap won't give us more credit on anything unless we pay off the feed debt." Carefully, she sipped hot coffee. "Can we get the rest of the west end watered today?"

"I was going to do that this morning."

"Take Chester with you. He can rail the new section. Where'd you leave the railroad tie?"

"Next to the corral." Chester, their hired hand, would hitch two horses to the heavy metal bar and drag it across virgin earth, flattening and clearing the land of sage brush, and afterward, plowing the scoured ground.

Aggie grunted in acknowledgment, then fell silent, eating slowly, her brow knitted, her eyes held steadily on her dish.

Aggie Tucker's high tan forehead was broken with thin arching brows above hazel eyes. Long salt

19

and pepper hair parted in the middle and worn loose was tucked behind her ears. She was lanky with a slight potbelly. Yet, at thirty-eight, she was still a strong woman. She wore a dress only for Sunday church service, otherwise preferring dark shirts, coveralls, and leather boots. When she was happy, she could be heard singing in a high soprano voice. When she had five minutes to spare, she read. Now she frowned — deeply, thoughtfully.

Sensing Aggie's rising depression, Nell reached out and put a hand on her lover's arm. "Hey, a little hope here, honey. We should just about make it this year."

Aggie slammed down her fork. "I don't want to *just about* make it, Nell. We haven't come close to making it in the six years we've owned this land. In fact, this year we've come closer to losing everything! So when are we going to *make* it? I don't want to end up working in Boise, again."

A dozen years ago, Nell's parents had moved from Boise to Grassy Flats to try their hand at farming. Her mother had died eight years ago and two years later, her father. The farm then passed to Nell. She added Aggie's name to the deed, and with no regrets, they packed their few belongings and left Boise where they had been working at subsistence level as store clerks. The only good thing they had ever found in the city was each other.

"Check with Roosevelt," Nell answered. Having finished eating, she stood, refusing to get drawn into Aggie's despair. She reached for a wide-brimmed hat hanging on a nail beside the door. "When we win the potato weight contest, we'll have a hundred extra dollars. Do you know what a hundred dollars means in nineteen thirty-seven? A hell of a lot."

"I know that," Aggie said irritably.

Nell looked at Aggie with fierce determination. "We'll make a special area in the vegetable garden for the contest potatoes and tend it like a baby. We're going to win that hundred bucks this year, Aggie. We have Chester to help us. And we have until November to beat the pants off anybody around. At least we have next year's hay bill paid for. We know for sure the horses'll eat." She bent down and kissed the top of Aggie's head. "I'm going to town. Where's the checkbook?"

"On the dining room table," Aggie answered. She sighed and walked outside with Nell.

A large brown dog extracted himself from beneath the front porch. He stretched and scratched, then danced alongside the women as they headed toward the corral. A dozen pecking chickens scurried out of their way.

"Hi, Barney," Aggie said, bending down and petting his big head. "The oil in the truck needs changing, Nell."

"No oil left. Have Chester drain the pan and run the old stuff through cheesecloth again. We better not drive unless we have to. We need to be saving every drop of gas and oil we can. I'll just take a couple of horses today."

"You'll be all day going and coming back," Aggie said in a practical tone.

"Nah. It isn't six yet. I'll be back by eleven, easy."

Nell saddled Baby, the roan mare, and used

Except for Chester helping them, Nell and Aggie worked alone, never quite accepted into the community. Two women, contentedly single and always wearing men's pants were to be held in suspicion no matter how much they had given the town. Still, Nell liked Grassy Flats, likcd the folks, their strong ways, their strong wills, their determination to succeed no matter what. She and Aggie knew everybody for miles around and chatted with them all.

Nell tied the horses to the hitching rail and stepped onto the feedstore's loading platform. She shoved back her hat to cool her forehead. Big Toss Cassidy passed briskly by. "Morning, Toss," she said cheerily. Toss ignored her and kept on going. Nell looked after him, perplexed that he had not spoken. They usually exchanged a word or two. She shrugged. "Fight with his wife, I guess."

She stepped inside the feedstore's cool interior, the smell of fresh-ground grain strong and pleasant. Specks of dust floated through sunbeams streaming through the open double doors and windows. Her boots thudded softly on worn floorboards, kicking up little puffs of dirt and chaff with each step. She strolled over and leaned against a deeply scarred counter. From a breast pocket, she drew out the checkbook and called out, "Morning, Rap."

A stocky man dressed in gray pants and shirt came from the back room and approached her. "Nell," he said briefly.

"Come to pay my bill." She smiled and began writing the check. She had learned from her father that no matter how flat broke you were, no matter how much it hurt like hell inside to give money to

24

others while you yourself were near starving and broke, you gave what you owed with a smile. It was certain that the one thing she'd been able to hang onto through these bad years was her smile. At least that wasn't taxable, subject to mortgage payment, repossession or garnishing.

She signed with a flourish and handed the check to Rap. "I'll need a couple hundred pounds of grain, Rap. Put it on my tab. Got a black gelding out front. Load it on him."

Rap took the check and folded it in half, tucking it neatly in his shirt pocket. "Cash for the grain, Nell."

"Cash? You gotta be joking. Nobody works with cash this time of year."

"Cash."

She shook her head in disbelief. "My crop won't be harvested till fall." She felt stupid telling him this. *Nobody's* crop would be harvested until then. "I'm looking to get two hundred and fifty bushels to the acre this year. I'm good for the money."

Stone-faced, Rap repeated, "Cash."

She could feel her face burning, and it angered her. However, she politely asked, "Will a check do?"

"It'll do."

Nell was uneasy. Rap had never been brisk with her before. She smiled, paying him, not allowing him to know how much he had upset her. "How's Toss?" she asked, sliding the checkbook into her pocket. "Just passed him. He seemed in a hurry."

"Wouldn't know," Rap answered and turned from her, disappearing into the back room.

She gazed at the empty doorway, feeling his rebuff clear down to the pit of her stomach. "Ah, the hell with him," she muttered. "He's just cranky this morning."

She crossed the street to the Rock Wren Diner, owned and operated by Tessie and Dusty Benford. She would have a cup of coffee and a doughnut before heading back to the ranch. She at least had enough change in her pocket for that. She'd bring Aggie a doughnut, too. Aggie would yell at her for spending the money, but she would still eat the doughnut.

Inside, a spattering of men sat at tables to the left of the long narrow room and on stools at a counter to the right. Nell glanced at their plates. Coffee and doughnuts. Most folks could afford at least that much.

Nell greeted the men, glancing back at them as she passed by, wondering at their unusual silence. Had the whole town had fights with their wives?

She seated herself at the counter. "Morning, Jeff," she said to the town's banker to her right and reached for yesterday's *Daily News* brought in from Boise. She quickly flipped to the stock market report, then closed the paper on the depressing news before tossing it back on the counter.

Jeff Myers briefly nodded at her, then glanced to his right. He flashed a secret half-smile toward Mike Perry, the blacksmith and garage mechanic. As she had with Rap, Nell again experienced a sudden uneasiness. What was wrong with these people today?

She leaned forward to look more fully at the men who stoically stared straight ahead. "Howdy, Mike," she said to the short, powerfully built blacksmith. His deep blue eyes avoided hers. "Can you come out

26

to the ranch on Tuesday and check the horses' shoes."

"Can't," Mike answered without glancing her way. "Too busy with the cars these days."

"When can you come?" she asked. She signaled toward Tessie. "A cup of coffee, and two doughnuts, Tessie. One to go." Tessie silently moved away. Nell's eyes followed her. Tess was missing her usual smile today.

"Don't rightly know, Nell," Mike said. "It might be quite a spell. Everybody needs their horses and mules shod or their vehicles fixed."

"Next week, then," Nell pushed. "Just to check their shoes."

"Maybe." He threw some change on the counter and stood. "So long, Jeff. Come on over about nine. I'll take care of your car. See you, Dusty, Tessie." Others signaled goodbye as he left.

Nell turned her attention to Jeff. He strained his coffee through a heavy moustache, his shock of brown hair falling into his eyes. Carelessly, he brushed it back. His suit, already rumpled from today's rising heat, fit tightly around his tall, plump frame. In a few minutes, he would open the bank's doors. There would be a light flow of traffic, then the bank would remain empty until just before closing.

"Jeff," Nell said. She leaned toward him and spoke in a confidential voice. "It looks like I'm going to need a little help this spring. What do you think the bank can do for me?"

Barely glancing her way, he answered curtly, "Nothing, Nell. You've used up all your credit."

Nell's nostrils flared with anger. "Since when?"

Jeff pursed his lips. "You're past due on your mortgage."

Rising slowly to her feet, she said, "By one week, Jeff. That's all."

"Now, Nell," Jeff stood, too, towering over her. "Don't get all het up. Banks aren't a charity business. Money due is money owed."

"A hundred dollars one week late isn't going to shut down your damn bank, Jeff. That's all that's due you right now. You could loan me a hundred and never feel it. Look at all the farmers hereabouts who are in the same situation I'm in."

By now the men had stopped eating and were listening to Nell's whispered sputtering and Jeff's outspoken voice.

"You owe everybody else in town, too, Nell. The emporium, the blacksmith, the feedstore . . ."

"I paid Rap off."

"Doesn't matter. You've become too poor a risk. You'll have to settle the mortgage before you'll get another dime from the bank."

"The *whole* mortgage? You're talking ten years!"

"Take out a chattel mortgage. That'll get you a little. Not much though, I suspect."

She glared at him for as long as he stood there. Eventually, it was he who moved first, dropping coins on the counter and then leaving, bidding good day to the others as he passed them.

"*Everybody's* a poor risk," Nell shouted after him. "Every human being all over the whole damn world is a poor risk these days. Have been since you lyin' bankers closed the doors on us in twenty-nine. Now, how about the loan?"

The door closed, and he was gone.

"Nell." Tessie stood behind the counter nervously glancing around. "Nell," she whispered. "You want me to make your doughnuts to go?" Tessie's blue eyes were filled with tears. Despite always looking brutally wind-blown, her long, curly hair the color of new copper was held back with a green bow giving it some semblance of neatness. Her stark white uniform set off the paleness of her skin peeking through the mass of freckles plastered on her face and arms. "You want me to bag them up?"

Through the large front window, Nell watched Jeff Myers disappear across the street and down the wooden sidewalk toward the bank. "Ah, to hell with him!" she growled. "Yeah, to go, Tessie." At the cash register, Dusty wordlessly took her money and gave her the change. Tessie handed her a small sack. "Thanks, Tess. Be seeing you, Dusty."

Dusty remained silent as Tessie said quietly, "Take care, Nell."

In front of the feedstore, Whip stood patiently beneath the weight of the grain. Nell mounted up and adjusted her hat. She had planned to stop for a paper, but she would forget it today. She felt sick to her stomach, not understanding everyone's unfriendly reaction. Folks had always been pleasant enough toward her. Doing business with them had never made her feel like a horse without a tail. The women often chatted with her, asking her how things were out on the farm, how Aggie was, and when Aggie came into town alone, how Nell was. She and Aggie went to their church; Aggie played the organ, had a choir, sang like a bird every single

Sunday. Everybody loved hearing her. They loved Nell's pumpkin pies and sugar cookies donated for bake sales every Christmas.

But today something was different.

Today, something was terribly, terribly wrong.

CHAPTER THREE

As Nell rode down the road, Aggie tossed cracked corn to the chickens and milked the cow, giving some to the cats and straining the rest, then storing it in gallon glass jugs in the cellar. Before calling Chester, she would straighten the house a little. Lord knew it could use it. Each spring, planting demanded every waking minute she and Nell had, leaving time for little else. Strangely, the look of a neat home made Aggie feel less anxious about money and the overwhelming urgency to get the potatoes in the ground.

She ran into the living room and flipped on the radio, then returned to the kitchen and stacked the breakfast dishes with those already filling the sink from yesterday's meals. She swept the floor and cleared the table, then wiped down the top of the woodburning cook stove. In the dining room, she folded and put away clothes that had laid on the big round oak table for the past week. She lowered the rolltop desk cover, hiding a shamble of papers, pencils and pens. With her hip, she closed the center drawer, left open since yesterday when she had hurriedly grabbed a pencil to jot down a note of something she must remember to do.

She returned to the kitchen and glanced at the wall clock. It was already after seven. She was worried about the growing lateness of the morning but went into the living room and refolded a blanket laying in a heap on the overstuffed couch. Two horsehair chairs, both graced with chimney lanterns on end tables, were the only items always left free of clutter. This evening, regular as clockwork, she and Nell would collapse in them. Maybe she'd dust the room and clean the fireplace later on.

Upstairs, she made quick work of straightening the bed and at the same time, considered doing a load of wash if there was still time left in the day. That would clear up the corner by the dresser. She remembered the long winter evenings when she had lazily sat reading or sewing or singing at the piano. She certainly could use some of that spare time now.

"I'm an Old Cowhand" came over the radio. Her spirits revived by her somewhat tidy house, Aggie hummed along in clear high notes as she walked to the phone attached to the wall near the kitchen door.

Ever mindful that there were seven other families on the party line, she carefully lifted the receiver off the hook, not wanting to interrupt someone's conversation, nor to listen in unless invited. Sometimes four or five women would be on the line at once gossiping like a flock of hens. She and Nell had both joined them from time to time.

Yes, someone was speaking. She started to hang up until she caught Nell's name being mentioned. Curious, she again pressed the phone to her ear, intending to join in. Recognizing Edna Vogel's voice, Aggie started to say hello, then heard Edna ask, "They were actually *kissing*?"

Aggie felt the blood drain from her face.

"That's what Thomas said. I made him stop talking about it," Florence Gordon answered righteously. "I always wondered about those two."

"Well, you should have let him finish . . ."

As carefully as possible, Aggie replaced the receiver as an unidentifiable noise roared in her ears. She staggered to the table and sank into a chair. Fear blanketed her. She tried to think but could only feel. Her breathing became shallow; her knees felt like water. She was sure that if she tried to stand, she would collapse.

She cradled her head in her arms and closed her eyes against the light of day and the words she had just overheard. She remained unmoving, her heart thudding in her chest. By now, the whole town probably knew the story. The kiss in the barn two days ago must have been observed by Chester. In a community as small as Grassy Flats, even with farms and ranches miles apart, gossip traveled faster than a lightning strike.

Aggie thought of Nell and wondered how she would make out in town. She considered going after her. Glancing at the clock, she knew she would be too late. Nell would already have arrived. But she wouldn't stay long. Someone would do or say something, and she would know something was up if not the exact nature of the problem.

Grassy Flats was not a forgiving town. Last summer, a bum had been nearly lynched. Someone thought he was doing some evil thing to a little girl when all he actually did was give her a piece of candy. Another time, the townsmen did in fact tar and feather a young fellow new to the area for stealing a hammer and saw from the hardware store. He'd wanted to build a shanty for his family. Maybe if he'd been a local man, someone who'd grown up here, who'd suffered through the Depression along with the rest of the town, Grassy Flat's cruel streak might never have surfaced.

Aggie and Nell had struggled through the early years of the Depression in Boise. When they came to Grassy Flats, they hadn't gone under as many farmers and ranchers had. The women were lucky to have inherited the farm. Two years ago, they had had money enough to hook up to the electricity put in by the state — not that they ever used it except for running the water pump to the bathroom and installing a single outlet to the living room so that they could listen to the radio from time to time. But if they had a good crop yield this year, they planned to extend the power to electric lights. They had dreams for this place. Maybe that was why Aggie had always felt an underlying current of resentment from some people — because she and Nell hadn't suffered unbearably with the town.

Oh, dear God, her heart cried out. Why? Why now? Why at all?

She sat up and wiped a sheen of sweat from her forehead. She must still call Chester, no matter what. She dreaded confronting him, even across the telephone wires. She remained motionless for several more minutes, going over in her mind exactly what to say, how her voice should sound. She would not let on that she knew what he had witnessed and that he had told it around. She would not let her voice quiver like the rest of her body. She would not let her tears, so near to bursting, flood her eyes.

She dragged herself out of the chair and walked rigidly to the phone. Cautiously lifting the receiver, she sagged with relief that the line was free. She cranked two long rings and a short and was put through to Chester's wife. "Morning, Sophie," Aggie said in a voice filled with an enthusiasm she did not feel. "Chester around?"

"Around and gone," Sophie Olmstead crisply replied.

Aggie sensed Sophie's coldness and leaned heavily against the wall. Of course, Chester's wife would know all the details. She probably knew how Aggie had pushed Nell down on the hay and kissed her as though she were never going to kiss her again; not just once, and not just on her lips, but after unbuttoning the shirt Nell wore, on her naked breasts. And Chester was one hell of a storyteller. "Is he headed this way?" she asked. "I should have

35

called sooner, but I needed to straighten up around here first. You know how it gets, Sophie." She was making conversation, trying to force Sophie to be her friend again.

"No, I don't know, Aggie. I seldom let things get in such a state."

No, of course Sophie wouldn't. She was never seen in the fields.

"Can't be helped right now, Sophie. We're all busy here. What time did Chester leave?"

" 'Bout an hour ago. He's in town getting the truck fixed. Appointment at nine, he said. Didn't expect to be back much before five today."

She was lying, bald-faced lying. Chester had promised Aggie two days ago he'd be here today. That had to have been before he saw her kissing Nell. "Tell him I expect him tomorrow, Sophie," Aggie said. "We have to plant that south end right away."

"He's tied up tomorrow, too."

"Doing what?" Aggie's temper began to rise.

"Didn't say. Just said he'd be busy."

"Tell him I called." Aggie replaced the receiver and returned to the table. Her hands clenched in front of her, she watched the skin around her knuckles turn white as she gritted her teeth and fought the rage within her against Grassy Flats.

How blissfully happy she and Nell had been less than two hours ago. Worried, yes, but happy. In past years, they had weathered many a storm together: broken bones, sickness, an operation for Aggie to remove a lump on her back, the intrusion of Aggie's mother's sister for a whole year that nearly drove Aggie and Nell mad and damn near drove them

36

apart. Somehow they would survive this too, Aggie expected. But this would be the tough one; this would be the storm.

She left for the barn.

The land was prime for crops, with a light soil and volcanic ash conditions containing a rich supply of trace minerals and enough acreage on the Abbott/Tucker farm to plow new ground every year if they'd had the equipment.

The farm's buildings were solid. The small two-story, two-bedroom white clapboard house, although fifty years old, was structurally sound. The big brown barn, just as old, was made of great oak beams and maple slab lumber freighted in from Oregon. A corral was attached to the barn. The buildings had withstood alternate blizzards and droughts with little damage. The outhouse stood comfortably near the house, converted to a toolshed now that the bathroom had been updated with a proper commode and hot and cold running water.

With shaking hands, Aggie harnessed a two-horse team to the wagon and loaded on a couple dozen milk cans. She was thankful for the hard labor she was about to face. It would help keep her from sitting around and brooding.

She drove over the flat, barren earth to a creek just north of their property line. The water, rapidly tumbling over rocks, tasted as sweet and cold as anything Aggie had ever drunk. There, she used a small portable trough she had brought along and chucked it under the creek's small waterfall, guiding water into each can. When they were full, she drank deeply from a dipper someone had thoughtfully left behind for others.

Harry Bibbs owned the land this water flowed through. Aggie toasted him for leaving this section to open range for everyone's use.

After the horses had drunk their fill, she drove to the field she hoped to finish plowing today. She unhitched the team and hitched up the single-bottom plow left there from when Chester had begun breaking ground the previous afternoon. She would use Tommy the bay. He was the more cooperative of the two horses, but only by a hair. Timmy, a dun, was tied to the wagon.

Aggie slung the reins across her left shoulder and gripped the handles. "Gitup, Tommy," she called. The gelding moved forward as Aggie guided the plow point into the earth and stumbled along behind the horse. Barring big rocks, Tommy's forward momentum would keep the point there until he reached the end of the row, five hundred feet away. Aggie would repeat the process until an acre was turned. Tomorrow Nell would plow another acre, and Aggie would drag this new section with a second two-horse team. The following day she would carefully plant a thousand pounds of seed potatoes exactly fifteen inches apart, in perfectly straight rows. This method would prevent the plants from producing too many leaves and too few tubers. She had learned from old hands in the area that planting closer or further apart reduced the yield of marketable potatoes.

The point struck a hidden rock and bounced over

it, painfully jerking her arms. Quickly, she drove the plow back into the ground, cursing Chester for not being here when she needed him. She was willing to bet he would never show again. The time had come, it seemed, to discuss renting George Applegate's tractor for a couple of days.

She was nearing the end of her eighth row when she spied Nell riding across the field on Baby.

Nell drew up and jumped from the saddle. She removed her hat and wiped her brow with her forearm. "Phew, it's hot today. Barney didn't even want to come along. Lazy dog."

"Smart dog," Aggie replied. "Cooler under the porch. How were things in town?"

They walked over to the wagon. Nell dipped into a can of water with a tin cup that hung from a nail beneath the seat. "I asked Jeff if he would consider loaning us a hundred dollars. He says our credit's no good anymore. Rap made me pay for the grain. Checking account's nearly empty." She looked over the rows that Aggie had just completed. "You plowing? Where's Chester?"

"He's not coming."

"Why not? He said he'd be here today."

"I called. His wife told me he had to take his truck to Mike Perry's at nine."

"That's funny. Mike told Jeff to bring his car around then. I didn't see Chester anywhere."

Aggie felt her stomach twist into a tight knot as she thought of how to begin. "Well, that's what Chester's wife said. Said he'd be busy tomorrow, too."

Nell cocked her head to one side. "Something's going on. Wonder what it is."

39

Aggie looked off into the distance. "Remember when I kissed you in the barn a couple of days ago?"

"Of course I remember."

"I'm sure Chester saw us. I overheard Edna Vogel telling Florence Gordon. They probably got it from Sophie who told —"

"Good Lord," Nell whispered. She slumped against a wagon wheel. Moments passed while she regained her composure. Suddenly angry, she said, "Well, so what? God almighty, Aggie, it's our barn."

Aggie moved to Nell and held her close. "But it's their community, Nell. Not ours. It's never been ours. We've just been tolerated, that's all."

Nell pulled away from Aggie and stalked off toward her horse. "I'm going after Chester and beat the tar out of him."

Aggie raced after her, grabbing her by the arm and spinning her around. "Oh, don't be stupid, Nell. In the first place, he'd kill you after your first swing. In the second, we aren't even supposed to know about this. And what would you say? 'I can kiss my woman in my own barn if I want to,' and then sock the daylights out of him? You can't say *anything*. You can't *do* anything."

"Then what are we supposed to do?"

"Take it! Take whatever Grassy Flats dishes out. We haven't done anything wrong. We're farmers just like the rest of them. We'll go on farming just like the rest of them. Act like nothing ever happened."

"Lord almighty!"

"We haven't changed, Nell. They have. To hell with them. To *hell* with them!" She didn't want to cry, but she couldn't help herself. She fell sobbing against Nell's breast.

Nell held her tight, her own tears flowing down her cheeks. "It's all right, honey. It'll be all right. We don't need Chester. We can make do."

"We need to rent a tractor," Aggie sobbed.

"I'll go see George today. Don't cry. Please don't cry."

Aggie wiped away her tears, then gently brushed Nell's face dry. "Were they nice to you in town?"

"No."

"That means everyone knows."

"Every blessed one of them. But Tessie spoke nicely to me. Seemed scared, though. And the men talked to me, but only to refuse me something."

"We've done a lot for folks here, Nell. We took Alice Smith's kid clear to Boise when he was sick. We loaned our horses when we needed them ourselves. We've given food, clothing ..."

"Wonder who'd help us if we got in a jam," Nell said.

Aggie breathed deeply. "We're in a jam, darling, and nobody's going to help us. I've got plowing to do," she said determinedly.

"I'll check on the tractor. Doubt I'll get it, though. I'll be back to water the west field in an hour."

Aggie looked deeply into Nell's dark eyes. "I'll remember these things, Nell, their treatment of you, of me."

"Don't, Aggie. You'll end up like them."

They parted, each with their shoulders squared against the day and the community of Grassy Flats.

41

CHAPTER FOUR

Tessie Benford plunged her hands into the steaming hot water and viciously scrubbed dried egg yolk from the white-glazed, thick china plate. She plunked it into a pan of rinse water and let the dish float slowly to the bottom. With a dripping hand, she brushed back an irritating strand of hair and tackled another dirty plate.

Her mind repeatedly relived this morning, her chest aching with grief and disappointment at the way the Rock Wren Diner customers had snubbed Nell Abbott. And the way Jeff Myers had treated

Nell had been downright shameful, deliberately letting everyone know how broke she was and behind in her mortgage to boot. And just who the hell wasn't these days? And all because Nell had kissed Aggie.

Tessie knew long ago that Nell and Aggie loved each other, probably a hell of a lot more than most men loved their wives. She realized it the day she had watched through the open door of the diner, Aggie helping Nell out of that rickety old truck of theirs and into the doctor's office after Nell had stepped on a spike, driving it up through the sole of her boot and out the top of her foot. After they had come out of the doc's office and passed by the Rock Wren with Nell limping along and leaning on Aggie like she was a tall oak tree and Aggie making like she was just doing Nell a casual favor, Tessie knew. She saw past the kidding Aggie was giving Nell, trying to keep up Nell's spirits. A puncture like that could cause lockjaw, and lockjaw could kill quicker than a cat. That's what had filled Aggie's eyes that day — the fear she might lose Nell. A friend you'd be concerned about, too. But a sweetheart . . . Tessie had seen it then.

Tessie softened as she thought of Nell's mouth always laughing through a heavy tan over strong white teeth, creases leading down from her nose to the sides of her mouth. The look of that mouth never failed to fill Tessie with warmth, though Tessie wagered Nell hadn't been smiling much lately.

Tessie had thought a lot about Nell since she'd learned about her and Aggie. At first she had been intrigued with the idea of two women sleeping in bed together. She had spent days dwelling upon the

43

very idea. She'd even thought about mentioning it to Dusty, but then kept her mouth shut, triggered, she guessed, by the powerful dream she had had not long after she'd figured out just what was going on out there on that potato farm.

Tessie couldn't even remember the dream anymore — just the kiss, the one between Nell and herself. That part she had never forgotten. It had been a powerful kiss, heated, full of passion, desire ... Every single love word ever used in those cheap romance magazines she read every once in a while applied fully to that single dream kiss. She had never experienced such a sensation when Dusty kissed her.

She leaped as Dusty put his hand on her shoulder. "Hurry it up, Tessie. You're dawdling, and I need you at the counter." Dusty was a small, thin man, his cheeks puffy, giving the impression that he constantly had a wad of tobacco stuffed inside each cheek. He was set in his ways and expected and demanded that things be just so. He was a creature of habit, and daily he wore a white shirt opened at the throat and rolled up at the sleeves, gray pants and a white apron. His socks and shoes were brown. Tessie suggested he change his wardrobe now and then, but it seemed that he couldn't unless he was going to work on the car. Then he wore brown pants and a white T-shirt and the same socks and shoes.

He rarely yelled or scolded Tessie, and he had never beat her. But he never let her forget that he ruled her.

Hastily, she finished the dishes and returned to the counter, pushing Nell Abbott and the dream kiss from her mind.

There were two things in Tessie's life that kept her from going insane in this one-horse town, a town she supposed was exactly like thousands of others scattered across the country, filled with citizens unbending in opinion, locked in what was right and what was wrong, allowing no possible alternatives in life.

Even though Tessie didn't stand much taller than five feet, she was so strong from carrying trays loaded with heavy dishes to and from the kitchen, she could drive a ten-penny nail into a two-inch thick board with a single blow. Her father had been able to do it, and as a child watching him, she had wanted to, too. She had practiced when he had, never being grown enough and then when grown, strong enough. But now she was both grown and strong, and when things got her down, like this morning's incident, at the end of the day when the diner closed she would go upstairs to the Benford's single-bedroom apartment and change into an old house dress, then go to the barn out back of the diner. Inside, she'd pick up a can of old nails, place a piece of scrap lumber astride two saw horses, and with anger bordering on insanity, drive the nails, one by one, into the board. When the board was full, she'd fill another and another until she either ran out of nails or boards or energy.

In the corner of the barn was a pile of mutilated lumber. Eventually, Tessie would use it as firewood, diligently recovering the nails from the ashes and using them over and over until the nails could stand no more pounding and no more fire. It was the one strange behavior Dusty let his wife exhibit, now and then insisting she display this unusual skill to his friends. He took bets on her abilities, pocketing the winnings. "See!" he would say as he collected the bets. "She's not only crazy, she's tough."

She wished he didn't call her crazy.

She supposed it was a crazy way to get rid of anger, but come the Fourth of July when the women were invited to drive twenty ten-penny nails straight into a three-inch plank, she'd be the one who won the ten dollars put up by the town's husbands and boyfriends just to see their womenfolk make fools of themselves in front of everybody. She hadn't lost in five years, and she hadn't given Dusty one penny of the money, either. The first time he tried to make her give up her prize, she threw a vase at him. She missed, but he never asked again.

That evening after the diner had closed and Dusty headed for his regular Thursday night poker game, Tessie went to the barn. Inside, the barn felt cool and smelled pleasantly dusty. Tessie picked up the nails and set up a plank. She *hated* the callous attitude of the customers. Bang! A nail sailed straight into the board with perfect precision. She *hated* washing stacks and stacks of dirty dishes. Bang! Another nail was buried deep within the wood. She hated the way Dusty treated her like a child. Bang! And called her crazy. Bang! Bang! The barrage against the wood continued until Tessie had emptied the can, and then she continued pounding until she had run out of grievances, her face contorted, the cords in her neck taut as hemp rope.

She gave the plank one final, mighty swing, then sank wearily onto an inverted milk bucket. Now she could face the bleak future again.

The second thing in Tessie's life that kept her

sane was hidden in a small metal box in the rock foundation of the diner. Only she knew its location and the dream that it contained. It had been passed to her by her father before he died. He had sworn her to secrecy regarding its contents. "Don't you tell anyone, honey, except your husband, and then not till you're good and ready. Promise." He had painfully gripped her wrist.

She promised.

She had never betrayed her father's confidence, not even when she had loved Dusty the most and wanted him to know everything she was thinking, what she was doing, where she was going that day, all that had happened to her. There were times when it was nearly impossible not to tell him about this wonderful thing that only she knew about, but she had always held back, reasoning that tomorrow would be soon enough to reveal her secret. Now there had been a string of tomorrows. Now she was glad she hadn't told him, for it was the one thing in her life that was hers and hers alone.

Maybe someday she would tell Dusty about it, and then he wouldn't call her crazy anymore.

CHAPTER FIVE

Outside the cab of the truck, the night was clear and cool. Brilliant stars blazed across the blackened sky, dipping down to the horizon of an even blacker earth. In the headlight's glare, the splat of bugs could be seen striking the window as Hank drove at breakneck speed over the unfamiliar dirt road. His mouth was drawn back in a grimace, his teeth bared. A wide hatbrim hid his eyes in dark shadows as he skittishly watched the rearview mirror.

The truck hit a deep pothole, nearly wrenching

the wheel from his hands, throwing him to the top of the cab. His head sharply struck the roof, and he let out a string of loud curses, fighting to bring the Ford back under control.

Clara was thrown painfully against the door. She stifled a gasp, grasping the door handle with one hand while protectively pressing the other against her stomach. She felt like she was going to puke again. Three days ago Hank had screamed at her when she had puked in the truck. He should have stopped like she had told him. Now she carried some paper bags, puked in them and pitched them out the window, knowing he would never pull off so she could have a minute.

Clara longed for this nightmare to be over. Wide-eyed with fright, she glanced through the back window. At any moment car lights would appear. This time Hank was running for his life, for *their* lives. There had been gunfire. If only he hadn't stolen the money and food from that grocery store; if only he hadn't hit the owner's wife when she started whimpering. Hank hated a whimpering woman. But the man hated his wife being hit more, and even with being threatened at gunpoint, he had flown into a rage, leaping at Hank, clawing at his throat and gouging his eyes.

Fighting off the berserk store owner, Hank had panicked, dropping the pistol and small bag of food. He bolted for the truck parked just outside, the engine running with Clara waiting at the wheel, wishing she were dead. Hank shoved her aside, took the wheel himself and raced away from the store. The bullets from Hank's own gun struck the cab, missing them but terrorizing Clara in a way that she had never known terror to exist. In less than a minute, she heard police sirens.

She wished fervently that they had already hit the Idaho border. There, they would be safe unless Hank broke into another store or got into a drunken fight with someone.

They had made it clear to Oregon from Chicago without trouble, Hank doing odd jobs, keeping them in gas and free meals offered by farmers' wives. They were going to stop in Bend and see her ma before heading down to California. But they hadn't been in Oregon an hour before Hank held up the store. The smartest and fastest thing they could do now was to run back to Idaho, away from Oregon's laws. It was damn unlucky that Hank had taken that wrong turn back there or they'd already be safe.

"Look at the map again, damn it," he shouted. "We gotta be someplace soon. There's only one bridge around here I know of, crosses the Snake. And hurry it up. I see lights coming up behind us."

With trembling fingers, she held a match close to the map on her lap. The road was so bumpy she could barely focus her eyes on the chart.

"Well?" Hank yelled.

Quaking badly, she held the light closer. "It looks like we might be here?"

"Here, where?" Hank screeched. "Where the hell is here? These sonsabitches are gaining!" Headlights grew larger in the rearview mirror.

"Throw the money out the window," Clara said. "That's what they want." Somehow Hank had managed to hang onto that.

"Like hell I will," Hank growled, and pressed the accelerator against the floor. The truck protested and groaned and then began picking up more speed.

"Where are we?" Hank demanded again.

"I think we're about a mile from the border," Clara answered, hoping this information would settle him down. He had thrust back his hat, his eyes wide and unblinking as he swiftly scanned the road ahead for the border marker and the Snake River that would separate them from their pursuers and guarantee their safety.

The car behind them drew visibly closer as Hank pushed the truck to its limit. Again Clara clutched the door handle and laid a protective arm across her stomach.

"There's the river," Hank cried triumphantly. "I beat 'em. There, you bastards, I gotcha now!" He sailed across the bridge and into the night. "We're home free now, Clara, old girl. We can relax." Hank smiled and began to slow down.

Clara turned and looked back. "I don't think so, Hank. They're still on our tail."

"What? We're in Idaho. They got no jurisdiction. Those varmints think they can catch old Hank Striker, they got another think coming."

He turned out the lights and floored the accelerator once more.

"Hank," Clara cried. "Have you lost your mind?" She could only think of her new baby, the one she hadn't yet been able to admit to Hank she carried, only recently admitting it to herself. It had filled her with joy and at the same time a terrible sadness. She didn't want to lose this one too.

"Shut up," he yapped.

A T-road loomed ahead of them, but with the lights off, Hank never saw it and zoomed straight across a crudely paved highway and into an open field. The bumps and ruts they struck threw them around in the cab like rag dolls. Hank refused to give up control and forced the bucking vehicle to keep rolling. He yanked the wheel to the right, the engine grinding, the truck protesting its forced path across the ragged earth. He drove for another half-minute or so and by some miracle, hit a dirt road with a gentle downward grade.

He shut off the engine, leaving the Ford in neutral. "Get out and push," he whispered harshly. "And keep yer damn yap shut."

They saw their pursuers stop at the 'T,' then turn to the left.

Unnecessarily, Hank said, "There they go. Beat them again, the dumb clucks."

Together, Hank and Clara rolled the truck down the road, not yet daring to start the engine, not knowing where they would end up, only knowing that it took them further and further from the law.

What difference does it make, Clara wondered to herself, that we got away? We'll only be running again in a week. Probably less than that. She was willing to bet her new baby's life on it. She was that sure.

An hour later they were on open road again. They had not seen another vehicle since they had hit this dirt road. As they drove south, Clara dozed fitfully, jerking awake every minute or so. She was worn out, thinking that she was fainting more than falling asleep. But she was too sick to her stomach to pay attention, whatever the cause.

Hank stopped by the road long enough for them to both relieve themselves before continuing on through the night.

Clara guessed it was about three in the morning when Hank said, "I gotta get something to eat."

A few minutes later they spotted a mailbox on the left, the first they had seen in several miles. He slowed and turned. "Might be a farmhouse up there. I'll see if they have chickens. Gimme the gun."

Fearfully, she uttered, "You dropped it back at the store, Hank."

"Naw, I got another one under the seat. Get it."

Her heart sank as she felt around beneath the seat. Hank had taken to carrying a revolver a month ago when he had beaten up a man who had tried to steal his hat as he ran past Hank. Hank chased the fellow, caught him and thumped him good. Searching the man's pockets, Hank had found a gun. Clara didn't know where he'd gotten the second one, only that he had it.

Her hands shook as she touched a burlap bag. She handed the weighty sack to him. "Is the gun loaded?" she asked.

He didn't answer, and she knew that it was. It was a wonder the pistol hadn't gone off during their mad ride across that plowed field. It was more of a wonder that Hank hadn't pulled it out during the chase and shot back at the police.

"Be back in no time," Hank said. "Turn the truck around and be ready to drive like a bat outta hell if we have to."

He faded into the night, and Clara dropped her head into her hands. Crying silently, she felt herself melt with fatigue and a near inability to move. She sat stock-still for two full minutes before sliding over to the driver's side to turn the truck around.

Clara sat bolt upright. She had dozed off but the sounds of pounding footsteps, galloping horses and a snarling, barking dog roused her in a hurry. She rolled down the window and looked out.

Running full tilt toward her, Hank was yelling at the top of his lungs. "Clara, get this heap going!"

With fumbling fingers she started the engine and turned on the lights. Reaching the truck, Hank flung something into the back, jumped onto the running board beside her and screamed, "Move it, damn it, get going."

Through the open window he repeatedly slapped her on the back of the head as she shoved in the clutch, unmercifully grinding the gears. A large dog growled and snapped viciously at Hank's trousers. After what seemed an eternity, the Ford began to inch forward.

"Floor it! *Floor it!*" Hank bellowed.

A burst of light and a roar exploded simultaneously. Clara felt her ears split with the noise.

Hank's curses and the smell of gunpowder filled the air as he climbed into the back of the vehicle. There was a single shot from Hank's pistol answered instantly with another roar from behind him. A slug thunked into the truck's side.

"Here, take your friggin' chicken," he yelled. He flung the sack onto the ground and turned his attention to Clara. "What the hell you doing, woman? Drive!"

Clara didn't understand what was happening. She had the gas pedal all the way to the floor, yet they were slowing down. Hank reached around and painfully dug his fingers into her shoulder. "Get going, I said!"

Hard as Clara tried to make the truck move, it continued to slow down. Finally, it sputtered and died. Hank leaped from the back, the gun still in his hand. He kicked at the dog snapping at his feet while the sound of hoofbeats drew his attention.

Just out of the truck's lights, a woman shouted, "Put down that gun or I'll blow your head off."

"Like hell," Hank rejoined. "Ain't no female tellin' me."

Instantly, a weapon went off behind him, hitting the truck, the noise as loud as a cannon.

"For God's sake, Hank," Clara pleaded. "They're all over the place. Drop the gun before they kill us."

From behind him came another woman's voice. "You're a dead man if you move an inch, buster. Sic 'em, Barney."

Hank threw his hands into the air. "He's already sicking me, lady. Call him off. *Call him off!*" Hank danced wildly, trying to shake the attacking animal.

"Come here, Barney."

Obediently, the dog backed away, vicious growls still rumbling in his throat.

Hank bent slowly to the earth, laying the pistol on the ground. "All right, I got rid of the gun, see? I ain't got anymore bullets, anyway. Now, let up.

There's your chicken. I flung it over there. It's still alive." Frenzied motion and wild cluckings could be heard within the bag. The chicken freed itself, frantically beating its wings and squawking wildly as it scrambled up the drive.

Hank spoke in a tightly controlled voice. "Now, folks, I can see you're mad as hell about all this, but me and my wife are damn hungry. You can't blame a man for wanting to feed his wife, can you? So I'm just gonna get in my truck and drive out of here easy like."

While Aggie continued to stay out of the glow of the headlights, Nell drew closer to the Ford. "Get away from that cab, mister." As Hank backed off, dull light gleamed off the twin barrels of a shotgun pointing straight at his chest. "You all right, ma'am?" she asked Clara.

Clara tried to make her hands move. She tried real hard, but she couldn't seem to make anything move. She felt sweat roll off her face and spittle dribble down her chin. Someone opened the door. She fell sideways and hit the ground with a thud.

She came to on a couch and rolled her head to one side. Hank sat rigidly in a straight-backed chair across the room from where she lay. Two women stood nearby. One held a shotgun on him; the other coldly eyed him before approaching Clara. She held a damp cloth in her hand. "Glad to see you're awake, ma'am."

Hank cried, "Keep your mouth shut, Clara. You don't have to tell them nothin'."

"My name's Aggie. This is Nell." Nell stood statue-like, her eyes fixed on Hank. "This fellow said you stalled the truck on purpose, Clara." Aggie gently placed the cloth on Clara's hot forehead. "He was very angry."

Hank mumbled incoherently.

"Where are you folks from, Clara?" Aggie asked. "You look a little worn."

"I'm going to be sick," Clara gasped.

Aggie grabbed a newspaper and laid it on the floor beside Clara who immediately leaned over. She had dry heaves going on endlessly. Finally she flopped back. She started to apologize, but Aggie shushed her.

Heading for the kitchen, Aggie said, "I'm going to get them something to eat."

"Oh, God," Clara moaned.

"Keep your eye on him," Aggie warned.

Nell nodded, holding the gun steady until they were called.

Assisted by Hank, Clara was led to the table. He was then made to sit alone and across the room. If he tried anything, Nell would have time to pick up the shotgun, already cocked and resting across her lap.

Hank began to wolf down bacon and eggs while Clara nibbled at oatmeal. "Don't you like oatmeal, Clara?" Nell asked.

"I do. I just haven't eaten much in a long time, and I'm feeling so sick."

"Shut up, Clara," Hank ordered. His plate was already empty.

Nell's face darkened. "You tell that woman to shut up one more time, Hank, and I'm going to smack you upside the head with this gun butt."

Aggie filled his dish again and slapped it down in his lap.

Hank fell silent and ate.

"Hank," Nell said evenly. "There's nothing that makes me hate a man worse than his thieving. Actually, it drives me a little crazy."

"You got your chicken back," Hank retorted.

Ignoring his comment, she continued. "And I bet I'm as poor as you. We have five hundred acres of land here, and it isn't earning us a dime. Fact is, we haven't made a decent profit on this farm all the years we've been here. So I really despise it when people steal from me."

Contemptuously, Hank sneered. "Yeah, and just how many have stolen from you?"

"Just you, so far," Nell answered. "And you can't imagine how enraged I am. I could kill you right now except for the mess you'd make in my kitchen. You'd have been smart to take note of the X painted on our front and back doors. Even a decent hobo would respect that mark and know better than to come begging and stealing at my door. I ought to shoot you."

Aggie grinned lopsidedly.

Hank's eyebrows rose in disbelief as he stared at her. "You'd let her shoot me?"

"Please," Clara whimpered. "No more shooting." She began to cry. "No more guns."

"You heard her, ladies. No guns." Hank looked hopefully at his captors.

"Till the sheriff gets here, there'll be guns, mister," Nell declared.

"No sheriff," Hank exclaimed. "I'll pay for the chicken, even though I let it go. Look, I got money." He hauled out a wad of bills.

Nell frowned. "Where'd you get that?"

"Honest work," he answered.

"I'll bet," Aggie replied.

"I earned it. Didn't I earn it, Clara?"

She lied. "He earned it."

Nell eyed the money, then glanced Aggie's way. "To hell with the money. It would be better if he worked that chicken off."

"Breakfast, too," Aggie nodded.

"Like hell," Hank muttered.

"You work, or you're going to jail, mister," Aggie told him.

"What would I have to do?" Hank asked. "And for how long?"

Nell looked intently at Clara, studying her.

Clara shrank inside herself, frightened of the women and of their gun ready to be picked up and used on Hank at any moment. She was puzzled at their kindness in feeding them. "Please, ma'am," she said to Nell. "We'll pay for the chicken. Just let us go."

"And we get to keep the hen," Hank said.

Aggie pursed her lips, inspecting Clara as Nell had done. "You don't look fit to go anywhere."

"It ain't anything," Clara insisted. "We just traveled too far tonight. We were going to my ma's in Oregon."

Hank nodded vigorously. "Yeah, that's right."

Before anyone could react, Clara tottered off the chair and onto the floor, unconscious again.

Hank leaped to his feet.

"Sit down," Nell roared. In an instant, the gun was aimed at his chest.

Wordlessly, he sank to the chair.

"I'll put her in . . . uh . . . my room, Nell," Aggie said, "and bunk in with you."

Hank's eyes widened as Aggie easily lifted the frail woman in her arms. Passing him, she asked sharply, "Don't you ever feed her?"

His eyes filled with bitterness. "With what?"

"You'll stay and work," Nell said, "until your wife is well. And you'd better not steal a thing from this farm or your life will be hell."

With no choice left to him, Hank reluctantly agreed.

CHAPTER SIX

The day broke cool and clear. At seven, Aggie delivered a second breakfast of bacon, eggs, toast and coffee to Clara who looked pale against the whiteness of the sheets. She stirred as Aggie shuffled things around on a bedside nightstand and placed the tray beside her.

Clara opened her eyes, betraying her fear of Aggie.

"Good morning, Clara," Aggie said cheerily. She opened the drapes and raised the window. A cool breeze caressed the room. "You slept like a log. I checked in on you from time to time, and you were really buzzing wood."

Clara sat up and wiped the sleep from her eyes. She smiled, pleasing Aggie. Aggie didn't want Clara afraid of her or of anyone. "I brought you breakfast. You just take your time eating, and get up whenever you feel like it."

Clara thanked her hostess and asked, "Where's Hank?"

"Nell put him to work plowing."

"How did she get him to do that?"

"Your truck's full of bullet holes. He can't drive away. If he walks off, we'll call the sheriff. He won't get far with that much cash on him. He's better off here. Where'd he get that money, Clara? He didn't earn it." All the while she talked, Aggie helped Clara sit up, fluffed pillows, handed her the breakfast tray, keeping her voice light and non-committal.

"Oh, he worked for it," Clara said, reaching for the coffee.

"How?"

"How?" The cup rattled against the saucer as Clara replaced it.

Aggie sat beside her on the edge of the bed and took Clara's hand in her own. "Clara, honey, he stole that money. He robbed a store in Oregon and flat out stole that money. It was on the radio this morning. They're looking for two gunmen in an old truck. They know they crossed the border last night, and they know they're in this section of Idaho. That's you two, isn't it?"

Aggie felt Clara's hand begin to tremble. "He . . . he'll kill me if I tell you."

62

"He needs to return the money, Clara, or the law is going to come sniffing around here, and you should tell him so. He could send it back through the mail. That'll keep them away from him — from you. That's all they really want, anyway. The money. It's what there's the least of these days."

Clara removed her hand from Aggie's and with both palms, covered her eyes. Her nails were bitten down to the quick. Dirt was ground deeply into her knuckles. The backs of her hands still carried last year's tan, as if she had rarely spent time inside a building. Dropping them, she said, "He hit a woman, too. The owner's wife, he said."

Aggie's lips tightened. "Does he hit you?"

"Sometimes," Clara barely whispered. "But he's a good man. He always finds us something to eat, a place to sleep."

"You call sleeping in a truck a place to sleep?"

"It's better than under a bridge. I ... I got to tell you, Miss Aggie ..."

"Just Aggie will do."

Clara smiled weakly. "Aggie. I'm ... I'm going to have a baby." She seemed to sag with her confession. "I'm about two months along, I think."

Aggie hoped her intake of breath was not detected. In her present shape, this woman could die trying to deliver — if she hung onto the child that long.

"I lost two. Hank never knew about either one. I lost them real early. I don't want to lose this one."

"Does he know?"

"No."

Clara's eyes were haunted. She reeked of dread and dismay. Aggie could have reached out and

63

touched the fear floating around her, could have grabbed handfuls of the stuff and molded it like putty, it was so thick.

"Eat," Aggie told her. "When you're ready, go take a long hot bath. I've put out a pair of panties if you don't mind wearing mine. There's a sundress and sweater in the bathroom for you. They'll be a little big. If you're up to it, take a walk around. Go on out to the corral and talk to the horses. They love people and follow them around like a bunch of puppies. And there's Barney, our dog. He hates your husband, but he'll love you."

"You sure it's okay?"

Again, Aggie took Clara's hand. "Honey, sometimes animals are better for a body than a human being could ever be. You could use some friends like that right now." She stood. "We'll all be back around six-thirty. We'll make dinner then. You eat anything you want today — and all you want. And drink lots of milk. There's plenty in the cellar."

Clara nodded appreciatively, and Aggie left her.

At the corral, Aggie bridled Sunset, the gentlest and prettiest of the six horses with a tan coat and white stockings and blaze. Clutching the reins and a fistful of mane, she grunted as she flung a leg over the unsaddled mare. Riding away, she saw where the crippled Ford had been towed behind the barn and out of sight of the road. Nell was determined to keep Hank here and had already shielded him from the law this way.

Arriving at the fields where they were working, Aggie saw Hank at the far end of a freshly plowed row, just turning Tommy around. Nell was working the next field over, methodically planting one potato at a time. Even at this distance, Aggie heard Hank curse as he tripped over something. She dismounted and tied Sunset next to Timmy already standing beneath a scrub tree.

Nell stopped and joined her. She freed herself from a heavy canvas potato sack hanging from her shoulder and the shotgun worn across her back with a leather strap. She rubbed both shoulders where the slings from the bag and gun had dug in.

"Think you need that?" Aggie asked, eyeing the weapon.

Nell wiped her brow with the back of her hand. "Today, at least. That man is angry. He cusses up one row and down the other, but he's doing fine. He's accusing us of blackmail. How's Clara doing?"

"She's all right. Worn out. I told her Hank needs to give the money back."

"He stole it, didn't he?"

"Just like we heard on the news."

Nell said, "Once he gets his truck going, if he does turn in the money by then, we have no way to keep him."

Aggie looked pensive. "If he cares one whit about that woman of his, he ought to stay through harvest time."

Nell shook her head. "I don't want him around that long. We can handle the harvest without him."

"Clara's pregnant."

"What?" Nell's eyes filled with distress. "How do you know?"

"She told me just a little while ago. She's not doing well at all."

"Damn!"

"Said she's already lost two."

"She'll lose this one, too."

"Not if she gets the right food and rest. Who knows how long she's been living like this?"

"Years, probably." Nell jammed her hands in her pockets, casting her eyes about as if searching for answers written in the sky or on the face of the earth. "And now you're talking two more mouths to feed for five or six more months . . ."

"We need Hank, Nell. He's all we're going to get. And his wife needs us. You going to turn her away?"

"Of course not," Nell replied tiredly.

"I never gave it a thought when I told Clara to make him give back the money."

Nell picked up the gun resting across the potato sack and looked toward Hank. "Then, we'll take it from him, and he'll have to stay."

A small gust of fear whirled through Aggie. "You sure this is the way to do it?"

"You got a better idea? You just said nobody from Grassy Flats is going to work for us. We're only going to get migrant workers — if someone passes through. Well, Hank here passed through, and this is the only way he's going to let go of the money." She clutched the gun in her hand, holding it before Aggie.

Nell was right. But what they were about to do was no better than what Hank had done, and that made the two of them no better than he. Aggie shivered at the thought.

Hank reached the end of the row nearest them and began to turn Tommy.

"Hank," Nell called.

Sullenly, he looked her way.

"Come here," she commanded.

He muttered something under his breath and pulled up the horse. He draped the reins around a handle and insolently sauntered over.

"Put your hands up," Nell ordered.

Hank spat and looked belligerently at his adversaries. "What the hell do you mean, put my hands up? I ain't took nothing."

"Put 'em up!"

Hank eyed the double barrels of the shotgun as his hands and eyebrows rose simultaneously.

"Clean out his pockets, Aggie," Nell said.

Aggie moved forward and reached nervously toward Hank.

"Get the hell away from me," he snarled. He grabbed for her hand.

"Don't move, mister." Nell raised the gun to her shoulder and cocked both barrels.

He froze, and Aggie, with pounding heart, rapidly rifled his pockets. She found the wad of bills she sought stuffed deep in his pants pocket and quickly rammed the money down her shirt.

"I'll get you bitches for this," he snarled. Spittle formed on his lips. "You're nuts, both of you."

"Now get back to work," Nell told him.

Aggie waited until she saw the plow moving forward again before saying, "I don't know about this, Nell. He's a mean one."

"We're just going to have to be meaner," Nell replied.

"You as sure as you sound?"

"Not likely." Carrying the gun loosely, Nell headed back to the field. Aggie followed, bringing along the potato sack.

Within three days, Nell's field was finished, and Hank's was plowed, dragged and marked off for planting. He was now using a two-horse team and going twice the speed that Chester had ever worked. Hank knew how to handle horses. He didn't abuse the animals, but he didn't favor them either, and they worked efficiently beneath his strong commands and firm control of the reins.

At six o'clock each evening, they quit. Hank freed the horses from field work and hitched them to the wagon. Aggie and Hank rode slumped against the watering cans in the wagon box, while Nell drove. The third evening the Strikers had been at the farm, Nell, Aggie and Hank found the kitchen table set and food waiting for them.

"Clara! How nice," Aggie exclaimed. "You shouldn't have done this."

"I wanted to, ma'am. You folks have been so nice to me and Hank here, and I'm feeling like I can do at least this much."

"Like hell," Hank interrupted. "Don't do nothin' for them. They robbed me. I ain't got one red cent on me. They took every penny and hid it someplace."

Clara looked with trepidation upon the two women. "When?"

Aggie went to the sink and began pumping water into a small pan. "First day you turned up, Clara. He should have told you right away."

"But the sheriff ..." Clara said.

"If the law comes, we'll turn in the money and say we found it," Aggie replied. She dried her hands and sat down. "Until then, if Hank doesn't pull his weight around here, we'll report him instantly."

Hank's face turned dark. "It's blackmail, Clara. Nothin' but pure blackmail."

Clara dropped her eyes, making no comment.

"Let's eat," Nell said. "Looks great, Clara." One by one the others washed up, then bent to empty the dishes of fried potatoes, sliced beef, peas, and milk.

Hank leaned back and belched contentedly. "Best meal you've cooked in a long time, honey."

"Give me a home, and I can cook like this all the time."

Surprised, Aggie looked at Clara. So the woman had some gumption after all.

Hank slapped the table, making everyone jump. "Shut your mouth, bitch."

Nell, sitting to Hank's left, slowly looked at him. She barely whispered, "I told you not to talk that way to her again."

Hank smiled defiantly at her.

Without warning, Nell slapped him on the back of his head. Across the table, Aggie and Clara froze.

"Ouch! Damn you, woman," he cried. He threw up his hands to ward off any more unexpected blows.

"Don't think for a minute I don't mean what I say. Don't ever make that mistake again." Nell quietly pulled the gun resting against the wall next to her side, then turned back to eating.

Scowling darkly, Hank watched her eat.

Clara fainted again, falling forward onto the table. Her plate clattered noisily on the floor.

With resignation, Aggie took her upstairs and tucked her in. "We're all just tired, honey," she said, wiping Clara's face with a cool cloth. "Don't think anything of Hank and Nell. They're just feisty, that's all. Nothing to worry about."

The look on Clara's face said she didn't believe Aggie for a minute, but she remained mute and closed her eyes, turning to the wall.

Rejoining the quiet couple in the kitchen, she asked, "Hank, do you know your wife is going to have a baby?"

Hank looked up from his plate. "Bullshit, she is."

"She's already lost two. Do you know that?"

"Like hell. She'da told me."

"She didn't," Aggie answered. "And you're going to kill her if you keep acting like a madman. You're scaring her to death. You better settle down."

Hank scrubbed his hands across his eyes. "Yeah? Well, you two are a bit worrisome too." His eyes shifted rapidly between the women. "When in hell are you gonna quit picking on me? I said I'd work, and I will, so put away your gun. But damn you, leave me *alone!*"

CHAPTER SEVEN

Alone at the kitchen table, Nell sat deep in thought, unblinking, her chin cupped in her hands. She should get up and go to bed. Everyone else was already there; had been for half an hour. She thought about Clara, assuming she was enjoying her second full week of sleeping in a bed. Nell hoped the frail woman would be all right and tonight had even sent her upstairs with a glass of warm milk. That's what she herself should have had instead of draining the coffee pot.

Thankfully, Hank was working out, cranky as he

was. He ate like a horse, but he worked like one all day long too, plowing and planting, and yesterday, shoeing the horses.

Living seven miles from town, owning only a single wagon and delivering no more than two 2,400-pound loads a day, Nell realized that come harvest time it was going to be mighty helpful having him around. He'd be able to spell her or Aggie, and they, in turn, could spell him. It would be an unpleasant job, the unpaved roads turning to muck before November, impossible conditions for a truck and strenuously difficult for a team of six horses working all day long, every day until the entire crop was delivered to the train station.

Nell rotated field usage carefully. Following harvesting, the ground was reseeded with alfalfa. Not until three years later did the alfalfa hay provide that field with enough nitrogen to produce another good yield. Lacking the element, overworked land frequently bore diseased and misshapened tubers unfit for sale.

This spring they were preparing several new fields. Thanks to Hank's superior ability in handling horses and equipment, they had a chance to produce a big crop this year.

Nell envisioned acres of green fields, of plants growing strong and healthy. The plants would need plenty of moisture, and watering them would be a tedious, time-consuming chore. The three workers would take turns hauling wagonload after wagonload of cans from stream to field every day after planting. With two handling a can, they would carefully soak the ground by walking between rows, slowly emptying the backbreaking containers.

But come November, when their crop was sold and they had won the potato weight contest, Nell and Aggie planned to pay off Hank, give the Strikers extra money to help with their baby, then send them on their way. The rest of the cash would be theirs. Nell's eyes gleamed with the possibilities of a profitable year.

Unconsciously, she rubbed her collarbone where the shotgun sling had dug into it for the last several days as she worked. After discussing it with Aggie, she had hidden the gun behind an old trunk in their upstairs closet. It was just too much trouble carrying the heavy thing, and she and Aggie were sick of worrying about Hank jumping either of them. He had said he would work. She decided to believe him rather than to lug that ironware around all the time. But its disappearance didn't seem to do a thing for Hank's disposition.

Upstairs, the bed creaked beneath her weight as she sat on its edge and pulled off her clothes, dropping them in a heap to the floor. She lay nude, contentedly listening to Aggie's steady breathing. Sighing deeply, she freed her mind of thoughts and concentrated on the noises of the house, heard it moan and shift. They were comfortable sounds, and they lulled her to sleep.

She awoke with sunlight streaming in her eyes and squinted at the clock. "Good Lord, six already? Aggie!" she yelled. She threw on her clothes and rushed down to the kitchen. There, she found Clara alone, setting the table.

Clara smiled brightly. "Morning."

Jamming her shirt into her pants, Nell anxiously asked, "Where are they?"

"Hitching up the horses."

Without the gun, Nell was still uneasy when either of them was alone with Hank. Nell hurried outside.

At the barn, Hank was buckling the last of the tack on Baby and Whip while Aggie calmly watched.

"Git over, horse," Hank ordered, giving Baby a shove with his shoulder until the stubborn animal moved closer to Whip. "Damn cussed animals," he muttered to no one in particular. He glanced at Nell as she hustled over.

"Morning, Nell," Aggie said. She chewed on a piece of grass. "Thought I'd let you sleep for a change."

"You all right?" Nell asked, glancing toward Hank.

"I'm fine."

Hank spat. "Relax, ladies. You worry too much." He backed the team to the wagon, efficiently hitching the horses to the tongue.

Nell started for the house. "Clara's making breakfast."

Aggie signaled Hank with her hand. "Come on, Hank."

Hank removed his hat and slapped it against his thigh. "Hell, woman, I guess I know which way the house is."

"Move it," Nell warned.

He glared at her, dropping behind them.

While discussing the coming day's work, they consumed stacks of pancakes and smoked sausage.

"Wish I had a tractor," Nell said.

"Rent one," Hank answered. "Then you won't need me."

"None to be rented."

"Bull!" Hank retorted. "This is potato country. Bet half the farmers around here have tractors. You could rent one at dusk. You could rent one part-time at least. Share crop. Everybody does it."

Quizzically, Clara looked at her husband.

"I know about farming," he told her. "I ain't always been a trucker."

"Where'd you learn?" she asked.

"Just watchin', you dumb . . ."

He stopped as he watched Nell slowly put down her fork.

"Sorry," he muttered. His gaze shifted to his plate.

Clara's eyes opened wide.

"What's the matter?" Aggie asked.

"He's never apologized before."

Hank leaped up. "What the hell do you expect? They got a friggin' gun on me all the time."

Nell rose too, speaking sharply. "Sit down, Hank. There's no gun on you. Save your energy for the fields. You're going to need it. And it won't kill you to apologize once in a while."

Clara sagged in her chair. Aggie reached out a hand, steadying her.

"We want to leave," the shaken woman whimpered softly.

"Yeah," Hank said belligerently. "Gimme my money. I'd rather gamble with the law."

"Not a chance, either one of you," Aggie declared.

"Clara, you'll never last through the summer. You'll lose that baby you're carrying, and Hank, we need a hired hand until this crop is in."

"In? In?" he screeched. "You're talking five, six months."

"Settle down then, and let's all work together," Nell answered firmly. "It's going to be a long six months. I don't like it any better than you, watching you all the time. It's worse than watching a baby. Barney has better manners than you."

Aggie flew into a fit of laughter that nearly made her choke before she brought herself under control. "I'm sorry, Hank." Tears streamed down her face.

Nell noticed Clara hiding behind her apron as though wiping her lips, but Nell knew that she, too, had been amused.

Hank sat smoldering. He quickly finished eating, then announced, "I'm going to work. Where the hell is the field? And don't forget your friggin' gun!" The room echoed with the slamming of the screen door.

"What made him so mad?" Aggie asked, and again burst into guffaws.

"I wouldn't poke fun at him too much, Aggie," Nell sensibly warned.

Clara nodded vigorously, looking very pale.

Between Nell, Aggie and Hank, they railed, plowed, dragged and planted steadily, carefully rotating the horses, while daily pushing themselves until time became a blur and worrying about Hank sneaking off with his wife in the middle of the night became a waste of time. Everyone slept as if dead.

And when they rose at five, the workers' backs still ached from the previous day's labors.

They were constantly hungry even though Clara kept them well fed, sending them with big lunches they consumed without thought and serving nourishing suppers they were almost too tired to eat.

Three exhausting weeks later, barely able to hold up her head at the breakfast table, Aggie pronounced, "I need a break. I can't stick another potato into the ground. Let's go to town."

Nell agreed instantly. She, too, had had it. They could afford to take one day off.

Hank's eyes closed with relief. "Thank God," he muttered. "You women are worse than a straw-boss."

"But I don't want to take the wagon," Aggie said. "And I'm not riding any horse. The truck needs to be run and the tank filled. The gas can too. It's almost empty."

Clara chose to stay, but Nell and Aggie insisted Hank come along. He seemed glad to join them. With Nell driving, they stopped first at Mike Perry's Blacksmith and Garage to fuel up.

The women ignored Mike's slow response as they waited beside the pump. Laying the money in his hand, Nell smoldered inside, his rejection of her and Aggie blatantly apparent. He doesn't know anything for sure, Nell thought, anymore than the rest of the town does. They only know what Chester's told them. Only after driving away did the rage within her subside.

They headed east, passing several farms whose horses, mules and few tractors moved slowly across the land. The musky smell of freshly turned earth drifted on warm currents.

Nell made a final swing toward Harry Bibbs' farm, located a little southeast of Grassy Flats. His fields, some lining the road, were finished. It looked like he had planted about twenty acres this year, apparently having just finished this morning, his tractor parked next to the highway, ready to be driven away.

"Rich bastard, ain't he?" Hank said.

"How do you know?" Aggie asked.

"Rubber-tired John Deere's a good tractor. Costs more than the steel-spoked wheel."

"Nice thing about a tractor," Nell commented. "You can put it away when you get around to it. A horse, you have to put away every night."

"Bet his cellar'll be packed this year," commented Aggie.

Beneath every grower's home was a potato cellar, a cool, dank room that smelled of mold and old dirt. It was there that potatoes were stored in field sacks until the farmer could rent Grassy Flat's community-owned potato sorter. Temporarily moved into the cellar, the machine was plugged into a light socket and potatoes were dumped onto its conveyor belt. With the room lighted by a bulb or two, working family members stood on either side of the belt. As the potatoes bumped noisily along, they were rapidly sorted and packed according to size into brand new one-hundred-pound burlap bags labeled "Idaho Potatoes."

Only number ones, the best, and twos, second best, were taken to the train depot. Culls, small and often misshapen potatoes, were tossed into bushel baskets and used either as fodder or for next year's seed crop.

At the depot, the shipper weighed the farmer's bags and paid him accordingly. The shipper also had a responsibility to the receivers on the other end of his line, and the growers knew that for every load they brought in, the man would slice open a couple of their bags, top, bottom, and sides making sure the contents within contained only ones and twos. It was possible to hide culls in the middle of a bag by first lining the bottom with ones, then inserting a stovepipe and packing ones around it and filling the pipe with culls. The pipe was then drawn out and the bag topped with ones and sealed. Unless he dumped the entire bag, a shipper never knew. Not many farmers tried stovepiping anymore. Those who did and were caught never sold another potato.

Nell said, "I'm going to see if Bibbs'll rent his tractor. We could drive it home right now."

"Don't!" Aggie declared.

"Why the hell not?" Nell argued. "I asked George. In fact, I asked everybody but Bibbs. He's money-hungry enough. It'd just be more cash in his pocket. I'm not proud."

"You ought to be," Aggie answered sharply. "We don't need him."

"Yes, you do," Hank said smiling.

"Shut up, Hank," Nell retorted. "This has nothing to do with you."

Hank did shut up, but his smile remained smeared across his face.

Nell drove them the three-quarters of a mile to Bibbs's home, stopping in front of a single-story white structure surrounded by a few thin, wind-whipped trees. A couple of barns stood out back of the house and a windmill off to the left. As they got out of the truck and approached the house, two ancient hounds resting beneath the trees announced them.

Bibbs came out immediately and stood on his wide front porch. He told the dogs to quit their yapping; they obeyed instantly.

Bibbs stood straddle-legged before his front door, silently studying the trio before him. He began to rock back and forth on expensive-looking black cowhide boots.

Harry Bibbs was a short, portly man with clean shaven rosy cheeks and eyes so pale a blue they resembled weak dish water. Thinning hair was combed across the top of his head, inadequately covering his nearly naked skull. He wore a black business suit with a gold watch fob across his middle. Looking superior, he said in a gruff voice, "Well, well, well. What a surprise to see you ladies out and around."

Nell refused to be intimidated. "Taking a break today, Harry." *He doesn't know for sure,* she thought. She said, "Looks like you're all done planting."

"We've moved right along this year. A tractor speeds up the work considerably. You ought to get one."

"Can't afford it," Nell answered. "But we can rent one. How about renting yours for a couple of days? I got an old mechanical plow somebody gave my father. I could open up new ground."

"Not a chance," Bibbs said.

"For a day, then," Nell countered.

He grinned. "Can't take a chance on it breaking down. Who'd fix it?"

"Hank here would fix it," Aggie told him, throwing a thumb in Hank's direction.

"Who the hell is Hank?" Bibbs asked. "I ain't never seen him before." Bibbs came over to the edge of the porch, his eyes raking the man. "Looks like trash to me."

"I ain't no trash!" Hank exploded. He charged toward Bibbs, then froze not a yard's distance from him.

From nowhere it seemed, a small handgun appeared in Bibbs's palm. It was pointed right between Hank's eyes. "Don't you even blink, bub," Bibbs whispered, "or I'll blow your useless brains out right here."

Without thinking, Nell stepped between them. "Back off, Harry. Hank works for me. You've got no call to act so uppity."

Hank slowly moved away, his teeth bared, his hands like claws as Bibbs raised the gun, slowly releasing the hammer before pocketing the weapon.

"Let's get out of here," Aggie spoke angrily. She grabbed Nell's sleeve and dragged her toward the truck, whispering sharply, "That was stupid stepping in front of that gun."

"He wouldn't shoot a woman," Nell argued.

"He'd shoot his own mother!"

Hank glanced back at Bibbs as he disappeared into the house.

Aggie scowled heavily at Nell. "Bibbs is meaner than a snake. It's a wonder he didn't shoot you!"

"I need a cup of coffee," Nell declared. They piled into the truck and headed toward town. Nell's face was flushed; sweat rolled down her cheeks, and her hands shook with anger and humiliation. *"Damn* him," she shouted, giving the steering wheel a sharp whack.

"Oh forget it," Aggie replied unsympathetically. "I told you so."

"I *hate* when you say that to me."

Aggie didn't respond.

Bibbs's refusal filled Nell's mind. Unable to let the incident go, she said, "Harry Bibbs can afford to rent his stinking tractor for a day! It wouldn't hurt him one damn bit to do us a favor for once."

"It will if you ladies make more money than him this year," Hank interjected.

"Wouldn't that really be something?" Aggie said. "Us outselling him. Bibbs beaten by two women —"

"And a man," Hank added.

"Yes, but two women . . . I'd like to beat his ass one time." Nell laughed wickedly.

Their mood was somewhat lightened by the time they had returned to town. Nell had at least stopped sweating.

Aggie led the way into the Rock Wren. Tessie was at the far end of the counter. Her hands filled with dishes, she could only smile across the room and call out hello, her face lighting up at the sight of them.

They had barely gotten inside the door when Dusty came from behind the counter and blocked their way. He first looked the women up and down, then scrutinized Hank. "You with them?"

Hank nodded, looking confused.

"Well, then all *three* of you ain't welcome here."

There was a loud clatter behind the counter as dishes fell to the floor, smashing to pieces.

Several customers observing the exchange from counter seats, started at the unexpected noise.

"What the hell you doing, Tessie?" Dusty yelled.

Tessie bent to pick up the broken plateware and was lost to sight. Loud indistinguishable mutterings could be heard as chunks of ceramic hit a metal waste basket.

Dusty again gave his attention to the trio before him.

Hank stepped around the women, "Just why the hell ain't *I* welcome here?"

Aggie reached out and stopped him. "Only because you're with Nell and me, Hank." She eyed Dusty angrily. "And it looks like he's madder than hell at us. So let's go. I don't want to cause any trouble."

"I ain't done nothing to you," Hank growled at Dusty.

"Come on!" Nell insisted, and gave Aggie and Hank a push toward the door before Aggie said anything more.

Dusty nodded in satisfaction. "You understand. Good."

"Like hell I do!" Hank flung over his shoulder.

"Take it easy, Tessie," Nell called out.

"See you, Tess," Aggie added.

Tessie didn't reply, but an even greater clatter of ceramic was heard from behind the counter as it collided with the bucket.

In the truck again, Nell pulled out onto the road and headed home. Hank's face was a black cloud.

"Forget the Rock Wren, Hank," Aggie said. "We owe them money, and Dusty's mad as a hornet because we can't pay him. He probably thinks that since you're with us, then you won't pay either."

Hank leaned out the window and spat. "From the looks of it, he wouldn't have given you a chance to pay up."

"He's real short-tempered," Aggie said.

Aggie's story was good, and Nell added to it. "It's a pretty big bill." She hated lying, and sensed that Aggie hated it as well. But their story seemed to satisfy Hank, and for that she was grateful. She sighed deeply. "Well, so much for the Rock Wren Diner."

"And renting a tractor," Aggie answered.

"And being trash," Hank concluded bitterly.

Nell shifted into third. "You're not trash, Hank. You're just a poor fool who doesn't know enough to relax and take care of a good wife."

"That all?" he asked.

"That's it," she replied.

"Just wanted to get your opinion right about me," he growled. "Least I got a wife."

Me too, thought Nell, and saw Aggie smile, knowing she was thinking the same thing.

CHAPTER EIGHT

Clara was awakened by a sharp nudge in her ribs. Hank whispered, "Get up."

"What is it?" she asked. The room was pitch black. Hank pushed her, forcing her out of bed. "What's going on?" she repeated. She heard him drawing on his bibs.

"Change your duds. We're going for a ride." He was still whispering, and she did too.

"We're leaving? What for? What time is it?" She reached for a bedside lantern.

The chimney rattled, and Hank uttered harshly, "No lights. Just get dressed. Be quick about it."

"Are we leaving?" she asked again.

"Yeah, we're leaving."

"What about packing?"

"Forget packing."

"We should tell Nell and Aggie. They count on us being here." Clara felt her knees turn to jelly. She couldn't possibly go back on the road. She was no longer strong enough to endure that kind of life. Not yet. Not before the baby was born.

"Hurry up," he ordered.

She did, fumbling in the darkness with her slip and dress buttons and the sweater she drew on. By the time he had pulled on his boots, she was ready.

At the bedroom door, Hank warned, "Not a sound." Quietly, he pulled it open, then led the way downstairs.

The steps creaked beneath their weight. At each noise they froze, Clara expecting Nell to come out shooting. She was touchy, that one. So was Aggie, but Aggie sang every once in a while, and Clara considered that a good sign.

They made it outside without incident, Clara breathing a great sigh of relief as she pulled the kitchen door shut behind her. Yet she was bitterly disappointed that the women hadn't stopped them. But why should they? They, like she, slept exhaustedly every night. Why hadn't Hank done the same tonight? It had to be a heavy thing weighing upon his mind to have kept him awake.

Hearing them, Barney came out from beneath the porch looking for a friendly hand.

"Go back, Barney," Clara spoke quietly. "Go on now." He padded back to his haven.

"Over this way," Hank said.

"But the truck's this way," she answered. Hank had worked on the Ford from time to time, but as far as she knew, it wasn't running yet. She tripped over some unseen object, stubbing her toe as Hank dragged her along with him.

They halted at the barn door before the Dodge. "Get in and steer," Hank told her. "Put it in neutral, but don't start the engine."

"You're taking *their* truck? You can't do that!"

"Get in and don't close the door," he said. "I don't wanna wake anybody up."

Breaking into a cold sweat, Clara obeyed. They wouldn't get out of the county before they were caught. Hank would go to jail for a long time. *She* would go to jail.

"Steer," he ordered. He put his hands against the door and pushed. The truck began to roll inch by inch down the drive, slowly at first, then faster as it picked up speed on the decline. Halfway down the driveway he jumped onto the running board and yanked open the door. "Move over," he said, bumping her hip with his own.

He pushed in the clutch and shoved the shifting lever into second gear, allowing the truck to roll all the way to the highway before slowly letting out the clutch. The engine coughed a time or two, turned over and carried them out onto the road.

"You'll never get away with this," she said.

"I ain't trying to get away with anything," he growled savagely. "But nobody calls me trash and gets away with it."

Bibbs! Hank had talked about the man all through supper. It was evident during her husband's babbling that he was far less angry with the Rock Wren Diner's refusing to serve him than with Mr. Bibbs calling him trash. Aggie had finally told him to shut up about it.

Clara could barely see Hank's face in the headlights' reflection, but she saw enough to know he was not going to be stopped from whatever he had in mind right now. She reached down and felt beneath the seat for a weapon.

"There ain't no gun," he said, startling her. "What I'm after is gonna fix Bibbs better'n a gun could."

Clara stared out at fields passing by that she couldn't see, fear making her fingers and toes tingle as though asleep.

Sometime later, Hank pulled the truck to a stop alongside the road. "Good. There it is, right where they left it this morning."

In the truck's headlights, she saw the tractor. Hank couldn't be thinking of damaging it, could he? "Whose tractor, Hank?" She thought she already knew.

"Bibbs," he answered flatly.

"Hank, please," she begged. Bibbs wasn't some town yokel. He was an important man. "You can't do this. Bibbs'll get you good." Her voice broke.

Hank backed the Dodge to the front of the tractor. From behind the seat, he removed a heavy chain. She wondered when he had put it in the vehicle. He had obviously peen planning this move all evening.

The dull metallic clink of metal against metal

was the only sound heard as Hank wrapped the chain around the John Deere's axle post and to the truck's bumper. "Get out and drive the tractor. Put it in neutral. I'll tow you."

She thought she misunderstood him. "I don't know how to drive a tractor."

"Well I ain't gonna have you drawing me," he snapped. "And I sure as hell can't start the engine and maybe wake somebody up, or I'd drive it myself, wouldn't I? You'd expect to hear car noises on the road at night but not tractor noises. Now get outta that cab like I told you, and get up on that seat. All you gotta do is steer."

"Where's Bibbs's house?" she asked. Where were his dogs? Everybody had dogs. And where was *Bibbs*?

"Way down the road. We're real safe. Nobody ever steals nothing around here, so nobody's gonna come looking."

She climbed onto the tractor seat, sick with fright. It was so high from up here. In a shaking voice, she asked, "Where's the clutch?"

He positioned her foot on the pedal. "Push it in."

She did and slid the shifting lever into neutral.

Fortunately, the tractor had been facing the direction Hank wanted to go, whichever way that was. Clara still didn't know what he intended to do with the machine. But he had been right about one thing: he was going to hurt Bibbs. To take a farmer's tractor was the present-day equivalent of stealing a man's horse. It had been known to get the thief hung. She shuddered at the thought.

"Don't oversteer the bugger," he advised, "or you'll dump 'er."

The John Deere's front axle was short, its small wheels positioned to within inches of each other, thereby balancing the vehicle on three points. At a fast clip, oversteering the tractor could easily tip it over, trapping the driver beneath its weight. Clara swallowed hard, bile threatening to pour from her mouth as visions of the John Deere rolling over her ripped through her mind.

Hank hopped into the Dodge and slowly eased it forward until the chain grew taut between tractor and truck. Clara felt a tug on the Deere. Struggling to hold herself together, she lessened the grip she had on the steering wheel and felt the ache in her arms recede.

They started rolling down the road, Hank keeping a steady draw on the chain. Clara fought to keep the tractor moving in a straight line behind him. Still, she weaved slightly from left to right. As Hank picked up speed, she used all her will power not to jump from the seat. She was convinced she wouldn't live to reach their destination.

He increased the speed yet again, and again Clara felt terror race through her. "Hank," she shouted. "Hank!" He either didn't hear her or was ignoring her, and they continued on.

A couple of miles down the road, Clara began to get the feel of the tractor. She was still scared to death, but she was doing better. She longed to look back to see if they were being followed, but she didn't dare divert her attention elsewhere. She'd probably roll the tractor.

It wasn't long before she realized Hank was heading back to the farm. She swallowed hard; he wasn't punishing Bibbs. He was punishing everyone:

himself, her, the women who had befriended them. Bibbs hated Nell and Aggie for whatever reason, and nobody liked transients. They'd all go to *jail*.

Sadness engulfed her as Hank finally slowed, towing her into the driveway and up the lane. Now they would be caught. Now the women would come gunning for them.

Lanterns came on in an upstairs bedroom. Seconds later, both women stepped out onto the porch, Nell holding the gun and Aggie, a lantern. Barney already waited for them, barking his head off at the strange vehicle.

Hank stopped before the house and turned off the Dodge. Clara slumped against the steering wheel, relieved to be here and relieved to see Nell put the gun back inside the house, having recognized her and Hank.

Aggie leaped from the porch, shrieking, "What in God's name have you two done?"

Clara stayed where she was until Nell, glowering fiercely, helped her down. She leaned heavily against Nell until she reached the porch and sank into a rocking chair. She barely managed to say, "He took Bibbs's tractor."

Nell whirled on Hank. "Who the hell do you think you are? Stealing *our* truck, using *our* gas for this *stupid* move! What was your next plan? Were you just going to park the tractor here and hope Bibbs or Aggie or I wouldn't figure out what you'd done? You're nuts!"

"Didn't have a plan," Hank said angrily. "Just wanted it to disappear. Thought I'd put it in the barn."

Aggie blanched. "*Whose* barn?"

91

Hank's eyes shifted rapidly from woman to woman. "Yours. He treated you like trash today too. I wanted to hide it in there just for a week or two to make things tough for him — like they are for me."

"Tough? *Tough?*" Aggie shouted at him. "You're eating, aren't you? You have a bed to sleep in, don't you? What's more, Bibbs doesn't even need the damn thing. He's all done planting." Her eyes were ablaze with anger. "Yeah, you sure made it tough on him, all right. I could bash your stupid brains in."

"Then you try being forced to work someone else's land day after day without wages and always being looked down on," he countered savagely. "That'll make a man nuts all right." He spat at her feet and sat heavily on the edge of the porch.

Aggie walked up to him, and without a moment's hesitation, slapped his face so hard his head snapped back. "We already told you you'd be paid after harvest, you ungrateful sonofabitch."

Hank stared open-mouthed at her, his hand held to his cheek, tears from the stinging blow glazing his eyes.

Clara bent forward, covering her ears with her hands. "Shut up, all of you," she shouted.

She waited for Hank to charge wildly into Aggie, but he merely looked at his wife. "What the hell's the matter with you?"

"I can't stand this fighting anymore." She began to sob loudly.

"We wanna be paid now," he said to his employers. "Me and Clara ain't seen a dime since we come here — 'cept for what you stole from me. That's theft."

Nell's face turned black as a thundercloud. "You want to talk about theft?" She jerked her thumb in the direction of the John Deere. "That right there is theft! Grand theft!"

Aggie disappeared behind the house. In seconds, she was back. "Here, damn you. Take your money and get out!" She threw Hank's greenbacks at his feet. "Get your truck out of here now. I'm done with you. Anybody who'd steal a tractor isn't welcome here. I don't care *whose* it is."

Hank scooped up the bills. "Come on, Clara."

"No!" Clara cried. She looked pleadingly at Nell. "Please, Nell. Don't let Aggie send him off." She must think first of her baby.

"They can't stop me," he retorted. "I can get the truck running."

Aggie ignored him and looked thoughtfully at the Deere. She walked around it a time or two. Abstractedly she said, "Go on, Hank," apparently having already dismissed him from her mind.

"No!" Clara violently rocked back and forth, her face buried in her hands.

"You're welcome to stay, honey," Aggie assured her, still studying the machine. "Isn't she, Nell?"

"Long as you want, Clara. But you, Hank," Nell said in a no-nonsense voice, "pack up and leave now. And don't even *think* of taking as much as a sliver from this farm unless it belongs to you." She detached the chain and climbed onto the seat. "Come on, Aggie, we've got to get this thing back. Bring the gas can from the barn. We'll fill the tractor once we get to Bibbs. Maybe he'll let us off if we do that."

"You're not gonna call the law?" Hank asked suspiciously, then quickly added, "Let's go, Clara." He walked off a few yards.

"Won't have to," Aggie answered. "They'll get you without our help. Hold on a minute, Nell."

"What do you mean, they'll get me?" Hank asked, rejoining the group.

Aggie turned to him, saying calmly, "The sheriff'll stop you —" She looked at her watch — "about seven in the morning. He goes by each day about then. He'll see a poorly dressed man, a stranger in these parts, pushing a bullet-riddled truck down the road while his wife, looking scared out of her wits, steers. He'll stop you and search you whether you allow him to or not because he has a big gun, and you only have a little gun and no bullets. Then he'll find the money. Now, how are you going to explain yourself?"

"You *took* my gun," Hank reminded her.

"You can have it back," Aggie said. "It's in the top drawer of the rolltop. The key hangs on a nail alongside the desk. Easy to find. Don't look for the bullets. They're long gone. Now, get off my land. I'm sick of keeping track of you and damned tired of listening to you whine all the time." She rested her hand on the rear fender and looked up at Nell waiting on the seat. "Nell," she said. "When Bibbs discovers his Deere missing, how long do you think it'll be before he comes looking here?"

Nell pursed her lips. "Right after daylight, I expect. Probably be the first place he'll think to look since we asked to borrow it only this morning."

Clara watched the scene unfold before her. Why were these women suddenly so calm? It was as if one were reading the other's mind. How aware of each other did two people become before their thinking became as one? She had never had a single thought that was similar to Hank's. She envied these ladies their closeness.

"It's nearly midnight," Aggie said. "If we worked straight through the night, we might be able to turn another two, three acres with that old plow of yours. Maybe even four if the gas holds out. That's all the land we'd really need planted to be sure of breaking even this year if something happened to hit the plants and killed some of them off. It'd be like insurance, you know? We could leave the tractor along the road about a mile from here when we're done."

"We'd have to allow time to wipe out the tracks," Nell said.

"Just drag the railroad tie up and down the driveway and over the road, then run the horses and truck over that a few times; make it look used. Beyond that, I wouldn't care if the tracks showed. Nobody's likely to drive by much before five. We could do it."

"Done!" Nell agreed. "We'd better move." Turning to the Strikers, she said, "You folks get along now. Remember, Clara, you can stay if you want." She climbed down and headed for the house, Aggie right behind her.

"Hank?" Clara looked desperately at her husband still standing there, the wad of cash clutched in his hand, his face working convulsively.

"Shit!" he screamed, flinging the bills to the

ground. "Shit! Shit! Shit!" He raged, kicking at the earth, dust flying everywhere. Barney scrambled under the porch. Hank cursed again, shaking a fist in the air as the others watched. Finally, he hurled himself onto the edge of the porch. "All right," he roared. "I'll stay. Doesn't look like I got any *choice*." His chest heaved, his breathing heavily labored as anger consumed him.

Aggie approached him. "I really meant it, Hank. I want you out of here."

"I'll go to jail!"

She pointed a threatening finger at him. "Then you better straighten up, because I'm sick of the sight of you. We need your help, but we don't need your dishonesty."

Clara dropped her face to her hands. She would be forever grateful to Aggie for allowing him to stay.

"We have plenty of gas including the Ford," Aggie said.

"You're not using any petrol from *my* truck," Hank protested.

"Yeah, Hank, we are," Nell replied. "Come on, Aggie. Let's get going."

Clara rose. She would pack them a meal and make sure every lantern in the house was fueled and ready for the coming nighttime work. Lightheaded, she moved toward the kitchen.

CHAPTER NINE

"Right there, right *there*. Yes. Oh Nell, where would I be without you?" Aggie dropped her thighs apart to more readily accept Nell's hot hand.

Nell shifted her weight, slid down Aggie's side until her cheek rested against Aggie's strong thigh. "You smell good," Nell muttered, pressing her face into the triangle formed by Aggie's hair.

"I love you," Aggie whispered. "I want you."

"You've got me, darling, now and forever."

Nell thrust her tongue into her lover. Aggie felt an ocean wash over her, electrically charged pleasure, wave after wave of giving from her cherished Nell.

Her climax hit hard, harder still because of the long time since she and Nell had last made love. She wanted to shout to the sky as she arched her back, wanted to rake Nell's back, clutch her until she crushed the air from her lungs. She did none of these things. She held Nell's head in place while gritting her teeth to avoid making too much noise lest the Strikers, sleeping just down the hall, hear them. She soared upward, upward until she could go no farther, felt she could stand no more. She squeezed her eyes shut.

Nell stopped moving, and Aggie sank into the mattress. She grabbed Nell to her and rolled over her. "Come with me, darling," she whispered.

Spreading Nell's legs apart with her own, Aggie positioned herself tightly against her lover's wetness.

They kissed, their lips blending together like the petals of a budding flower. There was nothing that was unfamiliar in the mouth of the other, yet they explored as though each kiss were new.

They began moving together, two intricate parts, two beings, separate, yet one, their understanding of exactly what each wanted, needed, tending each other, their rhythm practiced, their bodies slick with sweat and strong with the smell of woman.

Aggie buried her face against Nell's ear. "Take me," she whispered.

"I have," Nell whispered. Together their bodies arched against each other, their faces taut, lips drawn, jaws clenched. There was a gasp, a shuddering sigh, and they rested, tangled as tight as briers entwined.

In six hours they would get up and face the day. Until then, they slept peacefully, arms encircling each other, as if nothing could hurt them, separate them or conquer them.

"Never thought you girls would pull something like this! Stealing a man's tractor. Who's responsible?"

Aggie, Nell, Hank and Clara had gathered on the porch at the sound of the approaching vehicle. Even Barney had crawled out to sit beside them, his tail making soft tap, tap, taps against the boards. Harry Bibbs got out of his Ford and waddled up to them, his face contorted with anger.

Aggie listened with interest as he waved a threatening fist at them. She thought he would have shown up yesterday. When he hadn't, she and Nell surmised he had left the tractor where they'd dumped it yesterday morning just to see who might come along to drive it. She suppressed a smile, pleased they had outsmarted him. "We didn't take it," she said without guilt. But she was damned glad that Hank had. They had gotten three more acres plowed, and with the weather so dry, one of them was already dragged.

"Then why in tarnation was it parked only a mile down the road from here? You're the only farm around."

"Maybe you ought to put a guard on your machinery," Hank suggested. He smiled arrogantly, carelessly rolling a toothpick around his mouth.

"Shut up, bub," Bibbs growled. "You're just the hired hand here."

Aggie turned to Hank. "Hank, why don't you and Clara go inside and wait for us?"

Clara started for the door, but Hank hesitated. Impatiently, Aggie waved him on. All she needed was for Hank to get so mad at Bibbs that he started bragging about how he'd put one over on him; except it wouldn't go like that at all. Bibbs would want retribution and plenty of it. She breathed a sigh of relief when the kitchen door closed and she and Nell stood alone with Harry.

"You're lying, ladies. Both of you. I know you plowed with it," Bibbs said.

Nell stepped off the porch. "You're not going out to my fields to find out."

"Oh let him go, Nell," Aggie countered. "But be sure to show him our worn-out horses on the way so that he'll believe we used them and not his tractor." Given the opportunity to see the animals, still a little thin from having worked so hard for so many weeks, maybe Bibbs would believe them. Otherwise, he was apt to bring back the law with a search warrant.

"All right," Nell reluctantly agreed. "The horses are in the back pasture, Harry. It's only about three-quarters of a mile walk or so. I'd drive, but I need to save my gas. Come on." She turned to go, and Aggie followed.

Bibbs stayed where he was. "I can see the horses from here."

"You can't tell if they're tired from here," Aggie said. "We'll take your car if you want, then we'll go over to the fields. I suppose there's no reason you can't see them. They're about a half mile from here. Well, a mile actually."

"Almost two," Nell corrected, apparently realizing what Aggie was up to.

"Right," Aggie conceded. "But that's only because you have to cross that one little arroyo up the trail and then cut back down to get to the fields. The ride across the arroyo isn't too rough on shocks, and the rocks aren't real bad."

"Except for one," Nell said.

"Oh, yes," Aggie said. "There's just that one big one you'll have to be careful of, Harry. But I think you could get around it with just about any car. Especially this one." She sauntered over and patted a highly polished fender. "Looks to be in great shape."

Warily, he eyed the women. "I know you're lying, but I'm not going to wreck my automobile to prove it." He climbed back into his Ford, grinding the gears before driving away in an angry cloud of dust.

Aggie and Nell watched after him. "He's going to get back at us," Aggie said.

"What can he do? We haven't got anything worth much if he wants to take something. I suppose he could burn down the house or the barn."

"Not Bibbs. He's mean, but not that mean."

"You said he'd shoot his own mother," Nell said.

"He's also sneaky. That's worse."

* * * * *

Hank hitched the team to the wagon as the two women loaded the milk cans into the box before heading for the stream. Between the three additional acres planted and lack of rain, it now took the farmers five full days to water the fields.

"Wish we could afford to irrigate," Aggie remarked, slinging one more can onto the box.

"Someday," Nell promised.

They began the drive and were less than a half-mile from the stream when Aggie said, "What the hell ..." She stood up, straining for a better look.

Nell, too, stared straight ahead. "Am I seeing things?"

"Wire!" Aggie exclaimed. "That sonofabitch has run barbed wire."

Hank, riding on the end of the wagon box, laughed softly. "Three strings. You'll never get through that."

"The bastard," Nell exclaimed. "That *bastard.* He can't do this to us!"

So this was how Bibbs had decided to get back at them. Because he owned the land adjacent to theirs, by rights he could fence it if he chose. Aggie could barely control her voice. "When did he built it?"

"We haven't been here in two days. I'd say then," Hank answered, examining the wire. He checked its tautness. "Good job."

Nell, too, tested the wire, bouncing her palm against the top string. "He must have hired plenty of men to get it up in that short a time. Well, it's not going to stop us. I'm going after the wirecutters.

Let's get the cans over the fence. Fill them while I'm gone."

She unhitched the horses and slung a leg over a mount, riding bareback to the barn. She returned within forty minutes.

Aggie held out her hand for the cutters, "Let me do it."

"We'll share the job," Nell said. "I want a piece of this fence. Stand back." As she clipped the first two strands, they snapped, pinged and wound back on themselves.

Hank idly watched. "Bibbs ain't gonna like you gals cutting up his fence."

"This place has been open access since God invented the earth," Aggie replied, taking the clippers from Nell. "And by cracky, it's going to stay that way."

She cut the final string, leaving the way clear for the wagon to pass through. Bibbs wasn't going to stop them from using the water, law or no law.

The following morning, they had just left the breakfast table ready to begin the second day's watering. The team and wagon were set to go. "Okay, everybody," Aggie said. "Hop on."

Before they had climbed aboard, Nell said, "Hold it. Car coming. Looks like the sheriff."

"That's trouble," Hank said. In a flash, he disappeared into the house.

Side by side, Nell and Aggie waited for the dusty Dodge to grind to a halt.

Aggie put a boot on the running board and leaned on the window. "Howdy, Bob. Fancy seeing you here. Why, Harry Bibbs. You back again?"

She stepped back as Sheriff Bob Miner unfolded his tall, lean frame from the vehicle to stand towering over her. A wide-brimmed hat shaded his piercing blue eyes and white shaggy mane. A badge was pinned to his red flannel shirt, and a holster containing a big .45 hung loose against black wool pants tucked into worn boots.

Bibbs, in his usual drab business suit, emerged from the passenger side.

Aggie and Nell instinctively drew together. Aggie shoved her hands into her pockets to hide their shaking. Nell had hidden hers behind her back.

Miner cleared his throat.

"Go on, Sheriff, tell them," Bibbs urged. He wiped his sweating brow with a white linen handkerchief.

Miner looked at the ground, clearly uncomfortable with his assignment. "Miss Nell. Miss Aggie. Got a bill here I got to give you."

"A bill?" Nell stepped forward.

"Damages to Bibbs's fence. He says you cut the wire."

"We did," Aggie readily admitted. "We need the water. He's fenced it off. We've had free access to it as long as this farm's been here."

"You ain't got it if he says you don't," Miner replied.

"Pay up," Bibbs declared.

"For going after water that's always been available to everyone?" Nell asked incredulously.

"For cutting my wire, damn it," Bibbs retorted. "You got to pay damages. That's the law."

Aggie put her hand to her forehead. In an instant, her head was splitting. Of course it was wrong to cut the wire. But they had had no choice. "How much?" she asked.

"Fifteen dollars," Bibbs said.

"Fifteen dollars," she exclaimed. "Where do you think I'm going to come up with fifteen dollars? Take your bill and stick it."

"Arrest them, Sheriff," Bibbs said, turning to Miner. "They refuse to pay." He put his hand on Miner's arm.

"Don't," Miner said, his eyes searing Bibbs. The much smaller man backed away.

"Sorry, ladies," the sheriff said. "You got to pay damages or go to jail."

"What about right-of-way?" Nell asked. "That land has always had a right-of-way."

Bibbs dug into an inside breast pocket and pulled out a thick sheaf of papers folded in thirds. "I showed the sheriff this deed, ladies. There ain't nothing in it about right-of-way. Now pay up, or you're going to jail."

"I ... we ... haven't got the money," Aggie said. She turned to Nell. She was frightened and saw that Nell was too.

"Look, Harry," Nell said, stepping forward. "Maybe we have something that's worth fifteen dollars to you. You want to look around?"

"Cash," he answered.

Aggie squared her shoulders. "We don't have it."

"Then I got to take you in, ladies," Miner said. "I'm real sorry."

Nell barely moved, her eyes riveted on Bibbs. "Yeah, I can see that, Sheriff."

Aggie took a deep breath, steadying herself. "Clara!" she called.

Clara must have had her ear to the door because she was by Aggie's side within seconds.

"Clara," Aggie said calmly, "the sheriff must arrest Nell and me."

"Why?" Clara whispered. Her eyes were round with fear.

"We owe Mr. Bibbs fifteen dollars. We don't have it, so we must go to jail. I want you and Hank to take care of things while we're gone. Water and grain the stock. Take care of the garden. Don't use Bibbs's water anymore. Hank can water the fields from the house well. I don't know if he can do it alone. He can try. Don't *you* be lifting any of those cans." She silently added, and don't let Hank steal the place blind while we're gone.

Clara nodded and scurried back into the house.

Miner opened the car door, and Nell and Aggie stepped inside. "Sorry for the hardship," the sheriff said.

"Aren't you going to handcuff them?" Bibbs asked.

"Oh for God's sake, Harry," Nell snapped. "We're not dangerous. We're just damn poor."

Red-faced, Bibbs turned away. Miner closed his prisoners' door and climbed behind the wheel.

From within the house came the loud voices of a heated argument. Before Miner could start the engine, Clara flew out the door and ran up to the car. "Here, Sheriff. It's fifteen dollars. Count it." She shoved several bills at him.

Aggie held her breath. Miner was sure to ask where it came from.

But Clara apparently had already thought of

that. "My mother died last year. It's my inheritance. I've been hanging onto it until I really needed it. Take it."

"Looks like my job here is finished, Bibbs," Miner said, tossing the money on the seat beside him. "You're free to go, ladies. Just watch you don't cut any more fences."

From the opposite side of the auto, Bibbs argued through the open window. "You don't know where that woman got that money. She's a transient."

Miner coldly eyed Bibbs. "She said she got it from her mother. That's good enough for me. Now get your ass in the car."

Grumbling, Bibbs did as he was told, and in seconds the vehicle was headed down the lane.

Aggie and Nell stood with Clara between them, their arms wrapped tightly around the smaller woman's waist. All three watched the Dodge recede to nothingness.

CHAPTER TEN

Although it was only six-thirty and church services weren't for another four hours, Tessie slipped quietly out of bed to dress. She was careful to behave as she would have any other Sunday morning. Dusty was never a churchgoer and took full advantage of not having to open on Sundays. He was unlikely to wake and ask why she was up so early.

Actually, she didn't give a hoot about today's services. She had a different purpose. She was going to drive out to Nell and Aggie's and let them know they still had a friend in town. She was also going to apologize for Dusty's hateful behavior the other day. She still flushed at the thought of his turning these good women away and even including their hired hand just because he was *their* hired hand. And what made her so damned mad was that it wasn't the first time Dusty'd embarrassed her, making her feel like she ought to apologize, and later always had, to somebody for some stupid thing he'd said.

She couldn't very well tell him she was going to call on the ladies. Instead, when she got home she would tell him she just hadn't felt up to church once she'd gotten in the car and gone for a short drive instead, for he was apt to hear she hadn't been to church. She didn't know how long it would be before he learned the truth — or what he would do when he found out.

Ignoring the possibilities, she donned a blue cotton print dress, stockings with seams only slightly crooked and a large straw hat flecked with small blue flowers and skewered with a long hat pin to unruly hair. A purse dangled from her arm.

Downstairs, she stared for a long time at the large, clear glass jar containing a half-dozen doughnuts. Should she take along two? Dusty would notice them missing. He knew where every crumb was in the place. She envisioned the look on Nell's face at the sight of them, and Aggie's too, of course. But Nell was the one she favored. Nell's smile flashed before her eyes, and like a thief, Tessie extracted two frycakes, quickly wrapping them in waxed paper. She'd lie to Dusty about their disappearance. That's what she'd do.

Fifteen minutes later, she was at the farm. She had been here a few times before but never for too long, the women always so busy that while they and she had chatted, she'd had to follow them around from spot to spot as they worked.

At the front door, she knocked tentatively. She was plenty early to be making a social call on a Sunday morning, but she had little worry she would interrupt either of them getting ready for church. It wasn't long after the rumors started that Aggie had phoned the preacher. She was no longer interested in playing the organ or in directing the choir, and she and Nell didn't show up again.

The door opened, and an unfamiliar face said, "Yes?" The woman was tiny and very pretty. Her hair was long, its golden tresses gleaming. In spite of her healthy color, she looked a bit drawn around the eyes. She was also pregnant.

"I'm Tessie Benford, a friend of Nell's and Aggie's."

The woman's smile, although sparingly given to cover her deteriorating teeth, was radiant. Her voice was low and unobtrusive as she said, "They're working out in the field. Would you like to wait inside? They may be a while. I'm Clara Striker. My husband and I work for the ladies."

Tessie hesitated. It was this woman's husband who had been thrown out by Dusty.

"I should tell you first then, Mrs. Striker, it was my man who insulted Mr. Striker at the Rock Wren Diner. I'm very sorry."

For a minute, Tessie thought Mrs. Striker was going to slam the door in her face. But then she said, "He had no call to do that."

Contrite, Tessie said, "You're right, but I can't stop him when he shames me, and many's the time I've apologized for him."

The woman pursed her lips, her brow furrowed in thought. "Come in, then. You can tell Hank when you see him."

Mrs. Striker no longer sounded warm, and Tessie felt betrayed by Dusty.

Inside, she glanced around the kitchen. As before, its homey look pleased her with its flowered print wallpaper, the shiny chrome pipe extending from the cookstove to the chimney. There were flowers on the table, lending brightness to the room.

"Have a seat," Clara said crisply. "There's coffee. Would you like a cup?"

"Yes, thank you, Mrs. Striker." Tessie sat uneasily at the table.

"Just call me Clara. It suits me better."

To Tessie, being waited on by another seemed almost sinful. She could not resist saying, "This is a real treat for me to have someone serve me, and better than I deserve," then added, "I'd like to say again, I'm sorry."

"You didn't do it," Clara answered. "Men have funny ways. Women don't always understand their ways." The edge had lifted from her voice, and Tessie felt some relief.

Hesitantly, Clara added, "Made Hank pretty mad. Might be best if you didn't say anything to him today, after all. He's kinda cantankerous." She joined Tessie with a cup of coffee.

"It'd make me cantankerous too," Tessie agreed wholeheartedly.

"I still wouldn't mention who you are just yet.

Guess I said you should earlier 'cause it seemed like somebody ought to pay for treating him bad. But like I say, you didn't do it."

Maybe it was the throaty way she spoke. Maybe it was that tiny yet brilliant smile that accompanied her words. But Clara caught Tessie's attention, and Tessie looked straight into her eyes and liked her — a whole lot.

She was jarred at her quick attraction to this newcomer. It was almost like what she felt for Nell. No, it was *very much* like what she felt for Nell. Did feelings for a body pop up that quickly? Were they triggered by some unexpected little thing that made no sense to your brain but sure did to your heart that laid in waiting?

Her sentiments for Nell had started with the dream kiss. With Dusty, it had been the way he joked with her the first time she met him, although those feelings didn't last through two months' time after he'd bounced around on her so. Now here she was, grabbed by a pair of blue eyes belonging to a farmhand's wife.

Tessie was no stranger to what she was experiencing. Since she'd been thirteen years old and liked her girlfriends much better than the boys ever had, she knew something extraordinary was happening. She never did settle unformed questions in her mind, never expected to, and she never changed the way she got to longing for some of the women she'd known over the years.

Succumbing to the pleasant sensation, Tessie thought a second time, Clara's pretty. "Have you been here long?" she asked.

"Few weeks."

"I haven't seen you in town."

Clara shook her head. "Haven't made it there yet. Nobody here goes to town very often. Too much time by horse. Too much gas by truck."

"Well, if you ever do come in, I hope you stop at the Rock Wren. Just don't tell my husband who *you* are."

Clara laughed quietly. "That's funny, not telling our men who you and me are." She laughed again.

Clara's eyes sparkled; Tessie felt herself sliding toward her. She glanced at the floor to see if her chair was actually moving. Both she and the chair were stationary. She felt lightheaded and wondered if she was getting sick.

"I'll visit sometime, if I can," Clara said. Shyly, she dropped her eyes. "But ... well, we're a little short of cash right now, and I ..."

"Just to say hello," Tessie encouraged. As though it did not belong to her, she watched her hand rise from her lap and come to rest on the table next to Clara's. Feeling like a fool, she cleared her throat, trying to bring some reality to the situation. Remembering the doughnuts, she extracted them from her pocketbook. "I brought these for the girls, but why don't you just take them and eat them and be still about it." She felt a little guilty, as though she were betraying Nell.

Clara put up a protesting hand. "Doughnuts. Oh my, I could never do that. I haven't had one in a long time, but just the same, I'll share with everybody."

Tessie could no more stop herself from warmly

covering Clara's hand than she could have lifted the house from its foundation. Once there, her hand felt glued to the woman's warm skin. "Share another time. Keep these for your very own. I'll come by next week and bring enough doughnuts for everyone. That is, if it's all right if I stop again." She'd steal what she needed — and to hell with Dusty.

"It's all right with me," Clara replied.

With effort, Tessie removed her hand. "Then eat these goodies. Every crumb. It'll be our little secret. Our *second* secret."

"I haven't got one secret that's mine," Clara said. "Hank knows everything in my head. 'Course, I never go anywhere but what he's right there with me all the time." She laughed nervously.

"Well, he isn't here now, so eat up."

"You have to eat one too."

"Don't mind if I do. Do you like to dunk doughnuts in coffee?"

"My ma told me it wasn't mannerly. But when she wasn't around to see, I always did."

They resembled two conspiring generals, steadily staring into each other's eyes as they bent over their cups and brought the dripping frycakes to their mouths.

Having obliterated all traces of the doughnuts, Clara rode with Tessie, bumping over the irregular land to where the others were working.

"They started digging a well a couple of weeks ago," Clara explained as they walked toward a large mound of dirt stacked beside a five-foot wide hole in the earth. "Everybody's been taking turns shoveling whenever they have the time. Watering the fields

114

takes up most of it, though. Looks like Hank's below now. The whole thing scares the dickens out of me."

"Hello, Nell," Tessie called out. "Morning, Aggie."

Both women were standing by a tripod of stout poles positioned over the hole. From its apex was attached a pulley through which was threaded a thick rope. Using the rope, Aggie hauled up a bucket of dirt tied at its end and emptied it onto the growing mound. She let the bucket drop back into the hole, the pulley squealing in the quiet air.

"Well hello there, Miss Tessie," Aggie answered heartily. "This is a pleasant surprise. What're you doing here? The church burn down?"

Clara peered into the hole.

"I came to tell you," Tessie said firmly, "that no matter what the rest of Grassy Flats thinks, you and I are still friends. Dusty and his cronies are wrong in how they're acting toward you two." She was surprised at how hard her heart was pounding. This was tough to say.

Clara looked quizzically at Tessie.

"Look, Tess," Nell said softly. She took Tessie by the elbow, leading her a few yards away. "I expect you've heard why we're being shunned. But Clara and her husband have no idea that we're being shunned at all, other than what happened at the diner the other day. We'd just as soon keep it that way."

"Of course. I'm sorry, Nell." Tessie realized she should have kept her mouth shut to begin with and just come to see the ladies for a friendly visit. They would have understood what she was trying to say.

Nell said, "I'd hate like hell to lose the only help

115

I've been able to scrape up around here because they heard rumors somewhere."

"I understand. Clara suggested I don't tell Hank that Dusty's my husband, either."

"Good idea." Nell patted her arm and moved back to the well.

Tessie joined her, peering into the hole. "He's down there pretty far, isn't he?" She could see the glow of a lantern and Hank's shadowy figure.

" 'Bout fifteen feet," Aggie replied. She dropped the bucket below.

Suddenly from deep within the ground Hank yelled, "Sonofabitch! Pull me up! *Pull me up!*"

Tessie was pushed aside as Nell threw herself to the ground and shouted into the hole, "Hank, grab the bucket!"

"God almighty, it's filling in." Hank's voice was filled with terror.

Horrified, Tessie and Clara backed way from the gaping hole as its sides crumbled and slid downward.

"He's got the bucket," Aggie exclaimed.

Clutching her hands, Clara leaned heavily against Tessie, uttering, "Oh my God."

Tessie held her tightly. "They'll pull him up in time, Clara. Just hang on. Here, sit by the wagon. I'll go help."

"Tessie," Nell called. "Get on this rope and pull. He's buried now for sure!"

Tessie quickly eased Clara to the ground and ran to assist. She grabbed the rope's end and pulled with Nell and Aggie. There was no movement, and they pulled again.

"Harder," Nell barked. "He's not buried bad, but he's been under a good minute."

They strained a second time, and again there was no activity.

"Move back!" Tessie ordered, putting herself in front. Farmers handling the rope or not, she'd carried enough trays in her life to develop the shoulders of a bull. She knotted her hands around the cord, its stiff fibers biting into her flesh. "Now pull," she commanded. Her arms bulged with knotted muscles, the veins popping up like rivers of hemp. She heard the squeak of the pulley. Through clenched teeth, she repeated, "Pull!"

Motion! The rope gave only a fraction of an inch, but it was something. "Again!" she said, giving the rope another mighty yank.

A groan was heard from the pit's bottom.

"I see his head," Clara cried out. Tense as a rod, she had come to stand at the well's edge, wringing her hands and brushing away tears.

Inch by inch, they drew Hank from the earth's grasp. Near the top, his rescuers grabbed him by the arms and hauled him over the side. They collapsed on the ground with him as he coughed and sneezed, still fighting for air and spitting out dirt, while they gasped for breath.

Hank finally recovered, and Clara hovered over him, brushing the dirt from his face and hair, asking, "Are you all right, honey? Are you all right?"

"It's nothin' but dust down there," Hank wheezed. "Who the hell witched this hole anyway?"

"I did," Aggie said.

"Well, you're damn wrong," Hank told her. "I

heard you gotta drill two hundred feet for water in this territory. Got that? Drill! Not dig! Two hundred feet!"

"The pull on the willow was strong," Aggie argued. "We could be right."

"Right or wrong, sister," Hank said. "Get yourself another fool." He stood shakily on his feet.

Clara tried to steady him, but he brushed her aside. "Lemme get some air, will ya?"

Tessie's brows knitted. What was wrong with this man? His wife was only trying to help him.

"I'll get you some water," Clara said.

"I'd rather have a beer," Hank snapped. "You got any of that?"

"You know we don't, Hank. I can stir up some switchel real fast."

"Forget it." Scowling fiercely, he started for the farmhouse, brushing the dirt from his clothes.

Clara began to follow, but Aggie held her back. "Let him go, Clara. He'll be all right."

"He's so mad," Clara said.

"He's always mad," Aggie said. "But he gets over it. He's all right. That's the important thing."

Tessie drove Clara back, picking up a grumbling Hank on the way. Nell and Aggie returned with the wagon. Hank sulked in the barn while the others gathered in the kitchen. "I'll make switchel and run a pitcher out to Hank," Clara said. "Maybe he'll feel better."

She mixed a double recipe of water, molasses, vinegar, ginger and salt. After delivering Hank his switchel, the women wandered into the living room and sat quietly enjoying a second pitcherful of the thirst-quenching drink.

Tessie asked the farmers, "Do you think you'll have a good crop this year?"

"I hope so," Nell responded. She rolled her glass between her palms. "We've got plenty of acreage planted."

"What scares us," Aggie said, "is not transporting enough water to the fields. We're out there six days a week and only just staying ahead. Used to be five till our water supply was fenced off. You probably heard about that. It's enough to kill my back, those milk cans are so godawful heavy. And today, we darn near killed Hank."

Nell added, "We need to irrigate like sane people do."

"We need to find a million dollars too," Aggie replied. "Neither of which is going to happen."

They fell silent, staring blankly at the floor or ceiling or their hands. Finally Tessie said, "Can you use water from the house well?"

"We're doing that now," Nell replied. "Takes a lot of trips back and forth each day. Bibbs's water was much closer to the fields. That made the job simple compared to what it is now."

Quietly, Tessie said, "They put that fence up in two days."

Nell looked sharply at her. "We knew that, Tess. Who exactly put up the fence?"

"And nights, too. They worked nights. The fence is over three miles long."

"Who did it, Tess?" Aggie asked.

119

"All the ranchers and farmers around here. They can still get to the stream, even if you can't. It was built like that on purpose."

Nell slammed her fist against the arm of her chair. "It's so damned cruel."

Clara asked, "How do you know who did it, Tessie?"

Tessie paused, debating whether to continue. "Dusty was in on it." She might as well tell them. Nobody in this house liked him right now anyway. At the moment, she didn't like him very much either.

Aggie shook her head. "We can't dig a well by hand, and we can't be hauling water cans back and forth all day long, six days a week like we've been doing. Not with this many acres. We need a waterbox."

"What's that?" Clara asked.

"A big wooden box filled with water that rides on a wagonbed," Aggie answered. "You put a hose at the bottom and drive between the rows, watering. You can control the pressure. You can control the flow. Should have built it in the winter instead of sitting around on my tail doing nothing."

Nell ran her hands through her hair. "We haven't built one before because we figured it took as long to fill cans when we didn't have as many fields planted as it would have taken to build a box."

Tessie leaned forward in her chair. "I think you could build one in no time if you've already got the lumber."

"In no time?" Aggie challenged. "Nothing around here is ever done in no time."

"In no time," Tessie insisted. She moved excitedly

to the edge of her seat. "Remember, you're talking to the female nail-driving champion of the county. Contest's the Fourth of July. That's three days from now, and I could use some practice." She looked at her watch. It was still fairly early. "You cut the boards, and I'll nail them together. I never miss," she added. She would love the chance to put her bizarre skill to good use instead of using it to vent murderous rage.

Aggie shook her head. "I don't know . . ."

"I do," Tessie said.

"We have the wood just sitting there beside the barn," Nell said. "Old scrap, but it'd work with plenty of tarring."

"And she is the nail-driving champion," Aggie added, looking at Tessie. "We've both seen her do it."

"What's a nail-driving champion?" Clara asked.

"Got some bibs?" Tessie asked. "I could work an hour or so. We could do this, ladies." She paused. "I owe you."

"No you don't, Tessie," Nell insisted. "I already said as much."

"Well, no matter. I can help."

Nell went to the barn to collect materials, and Tessie left to change.

Clara had moved to the kitchen. She was sitting at the table and made a little "ohhing" sound just as Tessie came in.

Alarmed, Tessie asked, "Are you all right?"

"It's moving," Clara whispered reverently. "Feel."

Tessie came to her side, and Clara gently placed Tessie's hand against the stirring life inside her.

Tessie knelt beside Clara. "Do you suppose I could hear him . . . her? May I listen?"

Clara nodded, and Tessie rested her ear against Clara's growing belly. She could hear a whooshing, surging sound, not at all sure what it meant. "I'm jealous," she whispered. She closed her eyes, feeling warm and protective as her ear absorbed the warmth of Clara's body. "I've never had a child. Never will."

Clara slowly stroked Tessie's brow, causing tears to spring from beneath her eyelids.

Tessie stood. "Thank you," she whispered to Clara.

With Aggie and Nell sawing and Tessie and Hank, who seemed to have fully recovered, driving nails, the simply designed waterbox constructed on the wagonbed was near completion in two hours. It was large enough to cut by half the traveling time to and from the well. In the fall, with the aid of ropes and horses, the box could be pulled from the wagonbed.

From time to time, Clara wandered out to watch and to bring the laborers more switchel.

"I'd better get back to town," Tessie finally said, wiping her dripping face. "My, it's a hot one today."

Inside, she washed and changed. Clara waited for her on the porch.

"It was real nice to meet you, Tessie. Thank you for the doughnuts."

Tessie smiled. "I'd like to come back next week, Clara. I'd like to know how you and your baby are."

Clara laughed. "Come back and see us, Tessie."

Tessie glanced at her watch. It was now noon. "Dusty will be wondering where I am."

She sang all the way back to town. She sang a

couple of old lullabies her mother used to sing to her. She sang because her heart sang.

Next week, Clara's baby would have ten dollars because she, Tessie, would win it for her at the nail-driving contest. Next week, the women would have extra doughnuts, especially Clara.

And Dusty could go pound salt.

CHAPTER ELEVEN

As Clara arose on this bright sunny morning, she felt wonderful for the first time in a long time. She was getting stronger, able to do more every day. Already, she had taken over the duties of milking the cow and feeding the chickens. Yesterday, she had thoroughly cleaned the bathroom and dining room; today she would mop the kitchen floor and dust the living room. She would also spend time weeding the garden. Good thing for that garden and the cow and chickens, or they would be hungry! There sure wasn't any money to buy store-bought food.

She was growing larger every day. She was sure that if it hadn't been for the constant attention of Nell and Aggie when they had first found her, she would have lost her baby months ago. If she had, she didn't know how she could have gone on. She never remembered wanting a child as much as she wanted this one. Once in a great while, Hank would ask how she thought the baby was doing. Occasionally, he'd lay his hand on her stomach to see if he could feel its movement. He didn't say much, but she could tell he was thinking hard about that little creature in there.

She got up before the others and dressed quietly. She made her way from the bathroom to the kitchen and then began breakfast. Even if Hank never said thank you, Clara knew the women appreciated her efforts.

Hank came in a few minutes later, quiet and relaxed. Clara had noticed that he seemed calmer these days, not so likely to snap at her and criticize her every little move. Maybe he was more concerned about how *she* was feeling and not so all-fired concerned about himself all the time. Or maybe he was finally settling in like she had done, no longer worrying that the women were going to call the sheriff. She was glad they had stopped threatening him. It used to terrify her to hear Hank and the ladies sassing each other. She was sure someone would get hurt before it was all over. As it was, nothing but a lot of words had ever passed between them.

Hank left right away, saying he was going to gas up Nell's truck and buy a part for his own. Not long after, Nell and Aggie strolled into the kitchen and looked out the screen door. "Did I hear a truck?"

"Hank took yours to get gas and pick up something for ours," Clara answered.

"Are you serious?" Aggie asked, the alarm in her voice evident.

"That's what he said. Said if he was going to borrow it, he'd better put gas in it."

Nell added, "He better not be gone longer than forty-five minutes or I'll think he's up to no good, especially since he never even asked to use it." She took a seat at the table.

"He'll be back," Clara assured them, but she saw worried lines crease their foreheads. And for Nell to even suggest that Hank might steal their truck made goosebumps rise on Clara's skin.

Aggie said, "You know that his using that money for gas makes us accessories to a crime."

"We turned into accessories when we took the money from Hank and again when we let Clara pay off Bibbs," Nell told her.

"Why'd you do that, Clara?" Aggie asked.

Clara cracked eggs into a pan. The grease popped. "I didn't want to see you hauled off to jail. What would become of me — of us all?"

"Why does Hank stay?" Nell inquired. "To tell you the truth, I thought he'd be long gone by now."

"He's counting on a big payoff the day you sell the potatoes. He talks about it a lot." To Clara, he constantly complained that he hadn't gotten any money yet, as though the women could pay him now.

Aggie raised a glass of milk. "Here's to a profitable future."

Hank was back in plenty of time, easing everybody's mind. Tension drained like water from Clara's body.

Nell licked the last crumb of toast from her fingertips. "How about coming to the fields, Clara? We're going to hill potatoes, but you can sit and read if you like. It's supposed to be cool today."

"I had planned on doing some housework." She began to clear the dishes from the table.

"You do too much housework," Aggie said, steering her away from her task. "Toss aside that apron, woman, and come with us. It'll do you good."

"But what about lunch and supper?"

"We'll eat sandwiches," Nell answered. "Go get your newspapers.'

Clara grinned, realizing how much she cared for these ladies. They knew when she should take it easy. They were even planning on taking her berry picking sometime. She might ask Tessie to come along, too. The thought made her tingle.

Tessie had been so nice to her, coming out on Sunday mornings for the past couple of weeks, bringing doughnuts each time and all her old newspapers. She had even slipped Clara ten dollars for the baby that she had won at the nail-driving contest — the one no one here even mentioned attending. Most folks celebrated on the Fourth of July, but these people just kept on working. Clara wondered from time to time why the women stayed so much to themselves. She would have loved to have been there to see Tessie win, but she didn't dare ask for a ride.

She and Nell sat on the wagon seat while Aggie and Hank rode atop the waterbox. They chatted amiably, Clara watching the two-horse team's big muscles pulling the wagon across the dry earth, and Nell's deft hands handling the reins with ease.

At the north field, Clara spread out a blanket in the shade of a wagonwheel and made herself comfortable. She began to feed bits of information to the gardeners as they prepared to work. "You know Amelia Earhart?"

"Great woman," Nell answered. "Flies across the ocean and such."

"Says here," Clara read, "she disappeared over the Pacific Ocean. July third."

"Nah," Aggie declared. "She's too good a pilot. come on, sodbusters. Let's get going." She passed hoes to Nell and Hank.

It was true about Miss Earhart. Clara had heard it on the radio a couple of weeks ago and had forgotten about it. They all listened to the radio for a little while each evening, the four of them enjoying "Fibber McGee and Molly" or "The Shadow" or "Bunny Berigan and His Orchestra." They loved the radio shows, but most often Clara was the one left listening alone while her companions fell sound asleep with their mouths hanging wide open.

She looked up from her paper. Hank had shed his shirt, taking advantage of the unusually cool air, while the backs of the women's shirts and armpits were drenched in sweat. There was also a dark streak of perspiration down their fronts. She questioned who it was that instituted such a bizarre rule that women must suffer from heat while men did not.

"Want to ride with me?"

She awoke with a start, not realizing she had fallen asleep.

Nell stood over her. "Sorry, didn't mean to scare you. I'm going to water the plants. Hank and Aggie will stay here and keep hoeing. You can ride on the wagon if you like."

Clara rose awkwardly as Nell helped her up. "I must have gained fifty pounds overnight."

Nell laughed, assisting Clara to the seat. "I'm sure glad to have a waterbox," Nell said. "Should have built it years ago, but who would have ever figured Bibbs to fence off water?"

"Men think different than women," Clara answered.

"They do more than that," Nell said, drawing alongside the upper end of the field. She jumped from the seat and with the hose, fed water into the first two rows of potatoes. "Men are downright cruel at times," she remarked. "What if I raised livestock instead of spuds? I wouldn't have enough water. The animals would've died because some dumb bastard was mad at me because I ..." Her voice dropped off into a string of curses.

If it had been Aggie watering, Clara was sure she would have heard the same words. How wonderful it is, she thought, the amount of care and understanding these women give each other. When one is weak, the other is strong. Mostly they were both always strong, but when the need was there, so were they for each other.

She observed Nell's strong arms as she led the team by their harnesses from row to row. Over the weeks, Clara had seen Nell and Aggie do a lot of hard physical work. She admired strength like that in women.

For several days, hilling went on, sometimes by using a single horse and plow to gently push the dirt against the growing plants, but more often by hand to be absolutely sure no light hit the tubers causing them to turn poisonous, green and useless. Everyone, even Clara, though it gave her the shudders, knocked plant-killing Colorado beetles from the leaves into small cans of kerosene. With such care, the plants stayed healthy. They would yield a bumper crop for sure.

If it hadn't been for the mortgage coming due, everything would have been perfect. Clara knew the payment was coming up. Before the Depression, people bragged about all they owned. Since then, folks talked about who had lost the most or who was about to lose something, and there was no shame in admitting it.

Hank too was darn near as broke as the women, hanging on to his last twenty dollars like a drowning man grabbing for a straw. Over the days, Clara had watched him shift the single bill from pocket to pocket, always making sure it was there, always making sure only he ever handled it.

She sat at the table this morning pondering these thoughts, the others having already left for the fields. The sound of a car coming up the lane drew her attention. She craned her neck to see out the window.

Tessie! With a grunt, Clara rose to greet her at

the door. "It's not Sunday," she bubbled. "What're you doing here? 'Course, you're welcome anytime." Her cheeks ached with smiling.

"Brought your weekly ration of doughnuts just like I promised," Tessie answered. She handed Clara a small brown bag. "Can't stay but two minutes. Dusty thinks I've gone up the road after buttermilk. He'd be mad as a bull if he knew I detoured a little. Especially here."

"Come in then, for a quick cup of coffee before you go." It was funny how Tessie made her feel so happy.

They sat at the table, and in record time, Tessie had downed her coffee. "Gosh, that's hot!" She wiped her lips with the back of her hand. At the door she turned to Clara who had followed her closely. "Wish I could stay," she said.

Clara gently put her hand on Tessie's shoulder. "See you soon?" she asked.

"When I can."

They drew together, hugging briefly. Clara closed her eyes. Tessie smelled of freshly made doughnuts. "Drive safely," she said.

Clara watched after her until not a speck of dust from her car remained in the air.

CHAPTER TWELVE

Nell and Aggie rested on the wagon's tailgate, taking a break from watering the fields, while Hank, a few rows away, checked plants for infestation. With a long stick, Nell drew dollar signs in the dust at her feet. "Mortgage is due."

Her voice edged with anger, Aggie replied, "I know the mortgage is due."

Nell surveyed the fields. "Too bad we can't get an advance against this crop. Damn! I wish we could get a loan." She drew another dollar sign and with her boot heel ground it into oblivion.

"Know anyone who still trusts us?" Aggie asked.

"Tessie seems to."

"I've noticed that, but she can't loan money."

Aggie's eyes swept across row after row of healthy vegetation. The plants were now three feet tall and a deep rich green, a striking contrast against the unwatered land surrounding them. "These fields are beautiful," she said. "Hard as things are, I'm glad I'm not in Tessie's shoes. I couldn't stand working regular hours, waiting on men, listening to their constant politicking and gossiping. Farmers and ranchers around here think they know how to run the whole damn country, and they'll tell anybody who'll listen."

"That's only each other, honey," Nell said, lightly whipping the air with her stick. "Anyway, forget them and forget the country. Our job is to grow potatoes and worry about money. That's plenty."

"We could sharecrop with someone."

"Who?" Nell asked defensively. "Besides, we've already done all the hard work. Anyway, I'm not willing to let another body onto our property. I already feel crowded enough with Hank and Clara living here."

"That settles it, then. I won't even suggest we sell a piece of land." Aggie laughed and patted Nell's arm. "I'm only kidding, honey. You look as stern as a preacher."

Nell's frown increased. "To sell one square foot would be to bring people closer. Even owning five hundred acres doesn't seem big enough." Sighing, she leaned against Aggie's arm, knowing she should quit worrying so much. "Maybe we could get together later. It's been a long time."

"Think the Strikers ever hear us?"

"I doubt it. Hank would've said something by now."

"I worry about it," Aggie admitted.

"So do I, but I try not to."

Aggie smiled. "All right, then, tonight we have an engagement." Thoughtfully, she rubbed her chin. "I've been thinking, Nell. I could sell my piano. That might pay the mortgage."

"Not your piano. You need it."

"We need other things more."

"Wait on the piano," Nell said.

"It's the first of August. The bank must be paid."

"A piano won't bring in enough."

"Then I'll sell my radio."

"Why are we talking about selling only your things? I could sell something. My china or my chair, maybe."

"Good Lord, Nell. I wouldn't let you sell your chair."

"I can sit on the couch. Or, we could sell the couch."

"No!"

The issue was still not settled when later that day they returned to the farm. At the sight of the unfamiliar car parked in front of the house, Hank disappeared into the barn, but the women recognized the vehicle immediately.

At the kitchen table, Jeff Myers sipped lemonade. He rose as they entered. "Good afternoon, ladies. Mrs. Striker has been taking good care of me while I waited for you." He toasted Clara with his glass.

Clara smiled with satisfaction.

"Do you know who this man is?" Nell asked, staring at Myers with deadly concentration.

"He said he was your accountant," Clara said, obviously not having been told the moneylender's true title.

"Like hell he is. Get out of my house, Myers, right now." Nell picked up his hat from the table and flung it at his chest.

He made a grab for it, barely catching it. Smiling pleasantly, he said to Clara, "It's been lovely, Mrs. Striker." His eyes narrowed as he directed his gaze toward Nell and Aggie. "Until the tenth, ladies. Not a day later."

Clara looked confused. "You're their banker?"

Nell pointed at the door. "Out, Myers!"

Not batting an eye, he warned, "Be on time, girls."

As he drove away, he left the women on the porch, cursing him for coming here and cursing him again for deceiving Clara. Barney stood beside Aggie, a low rumbling in his throat as he always had when his owners sounded angry.

"I *hate* that sonofabitch," Nell raged. "I *hate* him!"

Clara whimpered, "I'm sorry, Nell. I'm sorry, Aggie. He said he was helping you straighten out your finances. I thought he was your accountant, someone you trusted."

Rigid with anger, Aggie replied, "Not one damn bit."

Clara began to cry in earnest.

Aggie put her arms around the tearful woman. "It's not your fault, Clara. Here, sit down." She led Clara to the rocker.

Nell's voice softened. "Aggie's right, Clara. It has nothing to do with you."

Clara dabbed at her tears. "I had no idea."

"He's a sneaky damn devil," Nell said, staring at the dust settling from Myers' car. "Forget about him, Clara. Come on, everybody, let's go in and kill off that pitcher of lemonade."

Seated in the living room, Nell studied the room as if seeing it for the first time.

Aggie watched her, her eyes following Nell's. "What on earth are you looking at?"

"I was thinking about what we might sell in order to meet the mortgage."

"I thought we were just going to drink lemonade and not worry about things for five minutes," Aggie retorted. "That's all I'm going to do if you'll let me, so quit selling off the house piece by piece."

"Right." Nell leaned back and closed her eyes, her brain continuing to operate full force. Apparently Aggie had been thinking about giving up her piano for quite a while. She would never consent to such a move unless they were desperate, and they were that, all right. Nell rose angrily. "I'm going to weed the garden!"

"Wait until the sun goes down," Aggie suggested. "It'll be a lot cooler and easier to work out there."

But Nell had to do something. She had to move. She could barely keep from shouting out everything wrong with her life, with *their* lives: flat broke, considering selling precious things, even entertaining fantasies of selling land; and they were saddled with

a pregnant woman they could never turn out who
had a husband who, in spite of his hard work, was
still barely worth the air he breathed, as far as Nell
was concerned.

She jumped up and left the house. "Come on,
Barney," she called. The dog scrambled from beneath
the porch. "Good pup," she said, scratching his ear.

The big dog pranced and barked at her side.

"You don't care who I love, do you, boy, or what
I wear, or who my friends are? You don't even care
that I'm poor."

Barney barked again, his gyrations indicating
that all she said was true. He found a bush and
settled in its shade as Nell began to yank weeds.

Nell and Aggie were nervous as they entered the
bank. Dressed in their Sunday best, each clutched
her pocketbook and smoothed the front of her dress.

"We got took on your piano," Nell whispered,
pulling the door closed behind them.

"We got fifty dollars, that's what we got," Aggie
answered. "We're lucky it was that much. It'll have
to do."

Jeff came to the window. "Afternoon, ladies."
Deftly, he counted the bills Nell had wordlessly
passed him. "You're short," he said curtly.

Two women had come in and stood in line behind
them, barely nodding a greeting. Aggie leaned closer
to the window. "Why don't you just announce it in
the papers, Jeff."

Nell sharply nudged her in the ribs. Throwing
Myers out of their house was one thing. But they

were in his house now, so to speak, and Nell knew better than to aggravate the man.

Myers said, "I expected full payment, ladies. On time. That's why I came out to your place the other day . . . to tell you that."

"You came to harass us, Mr. Myers," Aggie answered.

The others looked at the floor or out the window, but it was evident their attention was riveted on the scene before them.

Quietly, Nell said, "You're deliberately trying to humiliate us, Mr. Myers. You know we're in bad shape, but everyone is now." Peripherally, she caught the waiting ladies glancing at one another, their barely concealed smirks deeply hurting her. She knew exactly what each was thinking: unless she were a man, she would never love another woman. *They* weren't in nearly as bad shape.

"The rest of the payment is due," he said. "I'll give you until five o'clock. Then I begin to draw up papers."

Outside, Nell said, "We have to sell the truck."

"Are you crazy?" Aggie answered. "We need it to get to town, to haul grain, to carry junk to the dump."

"We'll use horse and wagon. Horses don't need gas and oil."

"For crying out loud, Nell! We can't drive the horses to town every time we have to come in."

"A lot of folks do, and if we start early enough, we can." Nell sighed deeply. "You know the town would love to see us gone from Grassy Flats. Looks like they're doing it through Myers. He's probably met with the bank's Board, and this is the plan they

came up with. And you *know* who's on the Board —
half the town fathers, nobody who'd consider letting
us alone." Aggie's eyes filled with tears. Nell stood
as close to her as she dared. "I'm sorry, Aggie. All I
can tell you is that we have a truck, and we have
horses. We need the horses more than the truck. I
say, sell the damn truck."

They stopped at Perry's Blacksmith Shop and
sold the Dodge for fifty dollars with the
understanding that Nell would drop it off tomorrow.
Aggie'd follow with horses for the return trip home.

Before they left town, Jeff Myers had the rest of
August's mortgage.

They sat down that evening and listed other
possible items to pay September through November's
mortgage: Nell's china, their furniture with the
exception of the bedrooms and kitchen, a
Revolutionary War-era antique gun passed down
through Nell's family, no more than two of their
horses. The discussion was long and painful.

"We have nothing left to list, Nell," Aggie said
later as they lay in bed naked and uncovered in the
warm night.

"We have each other and a hell of a good crop."
Nell could see moonlight glistening off the chimney
lamp beside her. "In six weeks, we're going to begin
harvesting. We're going to be all right."

"Last year we planted less acreage and had more
hands to help harvest. We planted too big a crop
this year. Us and our stupid ideas! The potatoes are
going to rot in the ground, and we're going to end
up in the poorhouse."

"No we're not, Aggie Tucker. Those potatoes are
going to be harvested! All of them, even if we have

to work twenty-four hours a day to do it! And we're going to buy back everything we've had to give up."

Aggie burrowed her head in Nell's shoulder. "I'm telling you, Nell, I'm as low as I've ever been."

"Darling, don't talk so." Nell stroked her hair and held her tight. She rose above her and rested against her. "I love you, that's what's important. Nothing else is as important to me. Remember that, Aggie. Remember that always."

Sighing deeply and relaxing in Nell's arms, Aggie murmured something Nell didn't catch. But she recognized that Aggie seemed less tense.

Kissing her slowly, Nell ran her hand down Aggie's shoulder. She caressed her breast, tenderly running a finger around the rigid nipple.

Aggie shuddered. "It's been a long time."

"We've had a lot on our minds," Nell whispered. "Please, darling, don't think about anything. Just enjoy how good I make you feel."

Aggie squeezed her hand. Nell felt her relax further, sinking into the bed. She spent long minutes caressing Aggie's smooth skin, starting at her breasts and moving her hand to Aggie's thighs, running her fingers through the course curly hair between her legs, repeatedly returning to her breasts to begin again.

She whispered soft words into Aggie's ear and kissed her forehead and cheeks and lips. Aggie's breathing became steady and deep and even.

Nell stopped. Aggie had fallen asleep.

Nell was first insulted and then saddened. It was no wonder that Aggie was already dead to the world.

All they ever did around here was work their asses off — and worry. Nell didn't remember this kind of strain on them last year or the year before that. But then, last year and in previous years they weren't without a dollar to their names — nor shunned.

Nell moved away from Aggie. Tears rolled down her cheeks as she stared into the darkness. "At least we're not sick," she whispered. "And we still have each other."

She fell asleep nauseous with worry, her cheeks wet with tears.

Monday morning at six, Tessie sat at the table sipping coffee with Clara when Nell and Aggie came downstairs. Aggie grinned. "You're becoming a regular around here, Tess." Tessie had been here only yesterday.

Nell was relieved to see Aggie smiling. She had been so discouraged last night.

"Can't stay," Tessie said. "I only came to bring Clara some newspapers."

"How're things in town?" Aggie asked.

"The same as they've been since the first wagon stopped here in eighteen seventy-three," Tessie answered. "Can I talk to you two?"

"You folks gossip all you want," Clara said cheerfully. "I'll go catch up on the news."

Nell and Aggie sat down. "You ladies ought to return to the church," Tessie said.

"Ha!" Nell slapped the table.

"And why should we?" Aggie asked.

"Because our organ player hasn't hit a decent note since you left, nobody knows how to direct and that old Ramona Beckwith sings louder than anybody else. The choir's a wreck."

"That doesn't answer my question," Aggie said.

Tessie studied her friends. "The women in town have always admired your independence, though they've never said so. I even know someone who threw it into her husband's face once. Now you've gone off and holed up like a couple of outlaws."

Nell leaned back in her chair. "Grassy Flats thinks we're pretty bad."

"Oh, who cares what Grassy Flats thinks?" Tessie replied impatiently. "What do you expect in a narrowminded town like this?"

"But somebody keeps talking about us and talking about us and talking about us," Nell answered angrily.

"So come to church. Hold up your heads . . ."

"No one has ever seen me hang my head, Tessie Benford," Aggie said.

"Me neither," Nell added.

"Maybe not, but avoiding town is the same thing."

"We were in last month," Aggie told her.

"For five minutes," Tessie flippantly replied. "I timed you from the window."

"We won't kill rumors by coming to church," Nell answered.

"No," Tessie admitted. "But you'll show them you're not afraid of what they think, either."

Quizzically, Aggie studied Tessie. "Why are you

out here, Tessie? Exactly why did you come here today?"

"To try to make you come back to church and to town."

Nell looked thoughtfully at Tessie and didn't believe it was the only reason she was here. Tessie had been to the farm several times lately and not always to see her and Aggie. In fact, Nell didn't see Tessie every time she visited — but Clara did.

Tessie rose and pinned her hat into place. "I've said all I came to say."

"Clara, we're done talking," Aggie shouted.

Nell didn't think it took Clara long enough to return from the living room and guessed that she had taken in every word. Nell refused to fret about it even when Aggie looked at her with deep concern, apparently thinking the same thing.

A truck came up the lane as they all stepped out onto the porch.

"Uh oh," Aggie said. "Telephone company."

"This early?" Nell wondered aloud.

Hank, expecting breakfast about now, joined them from the barn as the driver got out of his truck. Showing a surprising amount of loyalty to Nell and Aggie, Hank said, "Is it time to borrow his tractor, too?"

Nell wasn't sure if Hank meant stealing the man's truck or just plain running him down with it. "No thanks," she said. "We knew somebody would be out. We haven't paid the bill in three months."

The driver, wearing a drab brown uniform, approached them. "How do, folks. Name's Josh Haley. I'm here to remove a telephone from —" He read from an official looking paper — "a Mr. Tucker. Knew he'd be in the fields right off and thought I'd better get here early."

"Good morning," Aggie said amiably.

"Morning, ma'am," he replied, turning to Hank. "Are you Mr. Tucker?"

"I ain't," Hank answered and spat.

"How are you this fine day, Mr. Haley?" Aggie asked, blocking the man's way.

"I'm fine, ma'am. Now if you'll just let me by."

"Did you have any trouble finding the place?" she asked.

Nell looked at Aggie. Had she lost her mind being so polite to a company man?

"No, no trouble, now if you'll just step aside."

"This job must be very unpleasant for you," Aggie said, persisting in carrying on a friendly conversation in spite of Haley's obvious impatience with her.

"Only when I'm delayed by folks who like to chat," he answered.

Hank took a position in front of Aggie. "Look, mister, she's just trying to be nice. The least you can do is tell her good morning before you take her telephone. You can do that, can't you, act polite-like and say you're real sorry to have to cause her this hardship? She's trying to stay real friendly to you, 'case you hadn't noticed." A stream of tobacco juice landed in the dust next to the man's boot.

Haley reddened. "Sorry, ma'am," he said, removing his hat to Aggie. "Didn't realize it was your telephone."

The others lined up beside her. Nell asked, "What difference does that make? You're doing a dirty job. You could at least not take so damn much pleasure in it."

"It's a job, lady," he said. "Don't nobody like a company man."

"And we're among them," Clara said, thrusting out her chin.

Nell stepped close to him. "Get your job done, Mr. Haley, and get off my property."

They parted to let him through. Aggie showed him to the telephone and stayed with him while he removed it.

As Haley came out, Hank said, "My wife's expecting. If she needs a doctor, and we can't get one here in time, I'm gonna hold you responsible."

Haley looked with nervous agitation at Hank, while the women studied their farmhand as though he were a complete stranger. Nell wondered what was making him stand beside them so strongly. Warning bells went off in her head, but she thrust them aside.

"Here, ma'am, sign that the telephone was in good shape when I took it. Otherwise you'll get billed for damages."

Aggie snatched the document from him, signed it and thrust it toward him.

Tipping his hat, he mumbled his thanks and hurried away.

Anger hung in the air like thick fog. Aggie had an ugly look on her face. "Why don't we just burn the place down?"

Tessie came to Aggie's side and encircled her waist with her arm. "You just hang in there, Aggie, honey. Things are never as bad as they seem."

"Like hell," Aggie exclaimed. She stormed into the house.

Tessie said a quick goodbye to the others and left, and Hank headed back to the barn while Clara followed Nell inside.

"Make some breakfast, will you?" Nell asked. She went upstairs where she found Aggie lying face down on the bed, crying.

"Come on, honey," Nell said, sitting beside her. She began rubbing Aggie's back. "We can't let things get us."

"Lord, no," Aggie cried. "Don't let anything get us. Not the town, not the church ladies, not the bank or the telephone company. Nell, they've all got us. Every last one of them."

Nell could not think of a thing to say or do that would make life better for Aggie. She couldn't even think of how to make it better for herself.

She lay down beside Aggie, took her in her arms and cried with her.

CHAPTER THIRTEEN

Clara grunted as she swung her feet over the edge of the bed and sat up. It was getting tougher every morning to rise. She rubbed her belly and smiled down at the baby she could not yet see and said, "Good morning, child." She felt it kick. "The same to you," she replied, and padded to the bathroom.

She was surprised that Hank was already up and gone. She was usually the first one dressed with breakfast waiting on the table when the others came down. She splashed water on her face and slipped into a heavy pink robe and a pair of old open-toed slippers that Aggie had given her.

From a bushel basket in the corner of the kitchen, she extracted several pieces of kindling and some larger pieces of wood and stuffed them into the stove. She wadded some old newspaper and tucked it beneath the kindling. Striking a match, she lighted the paper. In minutes, there was a comfortable fire eating away at the chill that now settled in the house each night.

She expected to find Hank sitting at the table, hunched over a slice of toast and jam, but the room was deserted and as clean as she had left it last night. There was no evidence that he had even cut himself a piece of bread. Maybe he had gone straight to the fields to begin harvesting; they were going to start today. But would he go without first eating or go alone? He never had before.

She stepped outside and scanned the area. Barney, snoozing in a tight ball on the porch, barely acknowledged her. She wasn't sure what drew her eyes toward the barn where Nell had towed the Ford the night it was shot up. It had sat behind the building since that time. A tinge of fear leaped through her as she walked over to check. The truck wasn't there! How could that be? Hank had worked on it from time to time, but she had never known him to get it running.

With her heart pounding wildly, she made her way back to their bedroom. The only clothing in the dresser was her own. A tiny cry escaped her lips as she ripped through the remaining garments, flinging them aside, looking for a sock, a shirt, *something* that was Hank's. What they owned together wouldn't fill a feed sack. What he owned alone, he could stuff into the front of his bibs.

Refusing to believe the calamity facing her, she returned to the front porch, searching for some evidence that Hank would soon return. In the barnyard, the lowing of the cow sounded incredibly loud. Nearby, the chickens cackled and pecked at the earth.

She walked down the drive on rubbery legs, with a terrible and overwhelming knowledge that Hank was not coming back ... not coming back ... not coming back. The words reverberated around the inside of her skull, each phrase intensifying in volume, feeding a violent headache that had begun when she had first spotted the empty space that Hank's truck, *their* truck, had occupied for so many months.

Oh God, she silently pleaded, don't be gone, Hank, please don't be gone. What would become of her, a deserted and pregnant wife? How would she live? How would she live *alone*? How could Hank just up and leave her with strangers? No matter how nice Nell and Aggie were to her, they were still strangers. They couldn't possibly understand her plight. She was going to be *alone*. They still had each other.

Clara walked and then tried to run, her unborn child making it impossible for her to do much more than shuffle down the drive, her toes painfully striking small stones in her path.

She began to cry, breaking into uncontrollable sobs as she scurried further and further down the lane, stupidly trying to catch up to a truck that was probably miles, counties away by now.

"Oh God, oh damn you, Hank Striker. *How could you do this to your wife and child?* How could you? How could you do ..." Her voice became weaker and weaker, trailing to a whimper.

She slowed to a walk, then stopped dead, staring with disbelief at the emptiness around her. Nothing stirred now — not a rabbit, not an ant. Nothing! There was no life to be seen except hers. Even the cow had stopped its lowing.

Hank had deserted her.

Far down the driveway, she turned back, tired, tired as she had never been tired before. Was it possible to feel more weary from no man in her life than from no hope? Or were they the same thing? She had no man, and therefore, she had no hope.

She was *alone.*

Now she understood his recent kindnesses toward her and his loyalty toward Aggie when the telephone man came. He was leaving; he could afford to be nice for a change.

But he was certainly acting normally last night as he rode her like a dog, panting and slobbering over her back, his rough, calloused hands painfully pinching her heavy breasts hanging loose in her gown, his hips ramming against her bottom as he said, "This is gotta last me for a while, honey. Uh, uh, uh ..."

She thought his words meant he was going to stop messing with her now that she was so big. It wasn't that at all. He had just plain used her. *Used* her. He had always used her, all their lives together, but never as deliberately as he had last night.

She cursed his soul to hell, gritting and grinding her teeth. Her sobs broke into long moans, growing into a screech as she cried her grief into the bathrobe she had rammed against her face. "Ahhh, I hate you, Hank Striker. I hate you. I hate you, *I hate you.*" Gasps clogged her breathing, and she thought she was going to faint.

She threw back her head, refusing to give in to the darkness threatening to envelop her. "Like hell I'll faint. Not over you, Hank Striker, you son of the devil. Don't ever, ever, *ever* come back, because I'll shoot you dead." She raised her clenched fist at the road, screaming at the empty ribbon of dirt. "I'll never tell my child about you. He'll never know your name, and I swear to God you'll never hold him. I'll tell him his father was a good man, a great man, the opposite of the likes of you . . ." Her voice died away as sobs tore through her chest.

Hank was gone.

Hank had used her.

And he had used up everything left within her.

When she reached the house, she was exhausted. With movements as sluggish as slogging her way through a barrel of molasses, she managed to put together the coffee pot. She sat at the table waiting for it to brew and buried her head in her arms. She felt as hot as fire; sweat ran from her hairline down her temples and neck, soaking the collar of her gown.

Nell came into the kitchen. "Sorry I overslept.

Heard something outside ... Clara, are you okay?"
Immediately, she knelt at the grieving woman's side.
"What on earth is wrong?"

"Hank's gone."

"Gone? Gone where?"

"Just — gone. Left. With our truck."

"So he finally got it going. He's just gone after
gas, Clara."

"No."

"Don't be silly. How can you be so sure? And on
what? With what? He *has* to come back. *Aggie, get
down here!*" She made a rapid tour of the house.
The silver was still in the drawer; the few coins in
the pewter cup in the corner of the hutch were
missing; so was his gun. He had apparently taken
nothing else — except his truck.

Aggie's hurried footsteps thudded down the stairs
and into the kitchen. "What're you yelling for? I
wasn't even dressed yet."

Nell announced, "Hank took off."

"*What?*"

Clara sat up. Her head weighed a ton. "His
clothes are gone, and so's the twenty dollars he's
been carrying. And ... he ... used me last night."

"Men use women all the time," Aggie said.

"But it was what he said while he was using me
... and what he's been saying lately. I never paid
any attention." Clara brushed at her eyes with a
heavy hand. "It was the routine, I think. Too much
work. And never any money. Never any *hope* of
money."

"We're going to have money," Nell vowed. "All we

have to do is sell our crop. It's the best one ever. Hank was going to get paid a fair wage."

"He didn't think so. I think when you started selling off your stuff, he got real worried. Said you'd be wanting to buy it back and then he wouldn't get paid 'cause all the money would be gone by then."

"Well, he sure as hell won't get paid if he isn't here," Aggie promised. "We'll give you his share."

Clara began to cry again. "He's going to be a father. Doesn't it even matter to him? Doesn't being a father matter to a man? It would to me."

"Maybe if you were a man, it wouldn't," Aggie said, setting out three cups and pouring them coffee.

Nell added, "Hell of a responsibility, a kid."

Bitterly, Clara asked, "You ever seen a man feed a baby? Or change a diaper? Men only begin to take an interest in their sons when they can haul their own load. They forget their daughters altogether until they can marry them off. I was hoping Hank was different."

"You're a dreamer, Clara."

"Shut up, Nell," Aggie scolded.

"Sorry, Clara."

Clara nodded, forgiving Nell. "I don't blame you for being mad."

"I should'a shot the bastard when I first saw him," Nell said.

Clara burst into loud sobbing.

"Nell!" Aggie said sharply.

"Sorry, again," Nell said contritely. "I just need him for a different reason than Clara does."

"What the hell does she need him for?"

"For God's sake, Aggie, he's her breadwinner."

"Not much of one, if you ask me," Aggie said. "Clara, we want you to stay here and work for us as long as you want. Isn't that correct, Nell?" Aggie looked right at her.

"Of course!" Nell agreed. "I never would have thought otherwise, Aggie Tucker, and you know it!"

"Oh, stop fighting, please," Clara pleaded. "He's my husband. I'm the one who's stranded."

"You're not stranded," Aggie assured her. "Not at all."

"You're going to stay and cook, Clara," Nell said. "And when it's time, you're going to have a beautiful baby. Those are your jobs — to cook and be a momma. Mine and Aggie's is to figure out how to get those potatoes in without Hank's help. It would have been tough even with him, but without him . . ."

"But you're arguing, fighting because of me."

"Oh hell, we do from time to time, Clara," Aggie said. "But not because of you. Anyway, it's good for us."

"Yeah," Nell agreed. "Clears the air. Like a good storm does. We're fine. It's just that, like you, we're in shock. You lost a husband. We lost our help."

"You can get someone else," Clara suggested. She caught the look of hopelessness that passed between the women.

"No, we can't, Clara," Aggie said. "No one will come to help us."

"Why not? There has to be someone looking for work."

"Not with us," Nell answered.

"Stupid fools," Clara said. "Everyone is stupid.

Everyone. Except for you two," she added. "And Tessie. I wish Tessie was here. She's kind and gentle. And she loves my baby." She pushed aside her cup and sobbed into her arms. "I wish she was here."

Nell said, "We could call her."

"No phone, remember?" Aggie replied.

"We could go to town to get her."

"Sure," Aggie scoffed. "Shouldn't take you long by horse."

"I sure could have used seeing her today," Clara sighed.

The sound of a motor attracted their attention. Nell walked to the door and pulled aside the curtain. "Well, here she is to answer your wishes. What'd she do, hear us fighting clear to Grassy Flats?"

Clara sat at attention, glancing at the door. "Tessie?"

"Yep!" Nell replied.

Clara reached into the pocket of her robe and pulled out a handkerchief. She rose from the table, dabbing at her eyes. "Tell her I'll be right down. I can't have her seeing me looking like this." She disappeared, waddling up the stairs.

She left the women staring after her. "Why not?" Nell asked, perplexed. "She let us look at her like that."

Aggie looked at Clara's empty chair. "We're not the ones who can heal her heart. Apparently, Tessie is."

Clara soon returned to the kitchen, pausing in the doorway. The others sat at the table.

"I heard," Tessie said. "I'm sorry."

Again Clara began to cry, and Tessie moved to

take Clara in her arms. "Everything's going to be all right, honey," she said, holding Clara close. "I promise."

"You got friends, Clara," Nell said. "Are you going to be here for a while, Tessie?"

Tessie nodded, rocking Clara in her arms. "For as long as Clara needs me."

"Then Aggie and I are going to the fields. We'll just grab a loaf of bread and some cheese. We'll fill our jugs at the outside pump."

Wordlessly, the two women left them.

CHAPTER FOURTEEN

"I don't give a *damn* what you think, Dusty
Benford. I'm going out to that farm this morning,
and you're not going to stop me. They've got a
pregnant woman out there — no phone, no vehicle
and no one gives a damn about them except me!"

It was late October. Harvesting time was in full
swing with everyone scrambling to beat the weather
that now threatened daily to change into a roaring
beast even though the thickening skies still held off.

Without Dusty's consent Tessie had, for the past
few days, gone to help dig potatoes for Nell and

Aggie for a couple of hours each morning. She never explained where she went and ignored his badgering questions. Last night after work, things had come to a head when she finally admitted what she'd been doing instead of helping him open up. It had turned into an ugly scene. Dusty'd never hit her before.

She rapidly pulled on a shirt and a pair of pants she rolled up at the cuffs, not caring if wearing his clothes made him angry or not. She grabbed her coat and a scarf and stormed from the bedroom.

The door slammed on his curses as she hurried downstairs to the car parked alongside the diner. She jumped in and started the engine.

As she began backing out of the driveway, Dusty unexpectedly opened the door, startling her. Instinctively, she pushed in the clutch, halting the car. In a vice-like grip, he pinched her fingers against the steering wheel and said ominously, "You're staying. You don't tell me what to do. I tell *you*."

She swung her purse against his hand. "Let go of me, you big bully." She let out the clutch. The car lurched with a jerk.

"Turn it off, damn you!" He yanked the wheel to the left. "You're not going."

The car swerved toward the building. She rammed the engine into neutral and pulled on the brake. Leaving the motor running, she got out and pushed him away from her and the vehicle. "You damn men," she yelled. "You all act alike. You all *think* alike."

Disbelief registered in his eyes as he protected his face from her flailing hands and threatening fingernails.

She was nearly crying and fighting like hell not to. "You order your women and kids around like they're chattel and treat them with the same respect I'd give a dishtowel. Well, I know what your game is, Dusty, you and the *boys*! For all your power, you're not going to drive those women off their land. They'll stay and fight, and I'll help them all I can."

"Like hell," he growled through clenched teeth. He made a grab at her and missed as she ran back to the car. She jumped in and with frantic movements, slammed the door shut and rammed the locks home.

She rolled down the window a crack wanting to make damn sure he heard her. "They're harvesting by hand, and that's why I help. There's no harm in that. You can slop the hogs by yourself for a change."

Dusty hacked up a big wad of phlegm and spit on the ground. Tessie nearly gagged. He said, "They ain't even got brains enough to use a chain link conveyor. Everybody digs potatoes with chains."

She screamed at him, "Remember, Dusty, how they've always borrowed somebody else's conveyor? Remember that? And remember telling me that they're not going to find a farmer around that'll lend them a conveyor or the potato sorter or anything else that'll help them out? You told me that not a week ago, Dusty. Not a week ago. Oh, you felt so good bragging about it. To you, it was some kind of a big joke. So they're left with a total of three women to dig, sort and bag by hand, and one of those women is about to have a baby."

"Where's that worthless migrant husband of hers?"

"He took off when the going got rough," she said contemptuously. "Ain't that just like a man? So there's just them, Dusty. You and all the rest of this town made damn sure they never got decent help all season."

"You bet your sweet ass, honey," Dusty told her. "We don't need *that* kind in Grassy Flats."

Tessie shook her head. "Judge and jury, huh? And so sure of yourself. Well, I never saw anything wrong going on, so *get out of my way!*"

He brought his face to within an inch of the window, his eyes hard and angry. Little veins threaded their way across the surface of his nose. Tessie wondered why; she had ever thought he was handsome. "We open in thirty minutes," he said. "We got men to feed. *Real* men."

"God forbid a *real* man should miss a meal," she retorted. "Will he swoon if he misses one? *You* feed them. I'll be back by noon."

"Noon? You said two hours."

With eyes full of rage, he yanked at the locked door handle as she backed out of the driveway. She tromped on the accelerator, clutching the steering wheel, and glanced into the rearview mirror. "Then you shouldn't have made me mad, Dusty." He couldn't hear her. She was already halfway down Main Street, and he was looking after her, shaking his fist.

She felt lightheaded, relieved to have gotten away, to not have given in to him as she had been doing forever. Her hands and legs trembled, and she longed to pull over until the sensation passed. But to do that would cost her time, time away from Clara.

She reached the farm just as Nell clucked the four-horse team into motion. By the end of the day, the weight of the wagon's load would require that many horses. If they were harvesting under normal conditions, it would take six horses to pull the loaded wagon home.

"Hey, wait for me," she called and ran to catch up. She already knew they had to cross the arroyo to reach today's field. It would be difficult to take the car as she often did. She hopped aboard, shoving aside equipment as the women greeted her.

Now that most plants had died, the waterbox had been pulled from the wagon. These days, the bed was loaded with bushel baskets, forks, a milk can of water to make up for when they ran out of switchel and lemonade and brand new hundred-pound shipping bags with Idaho Potatoes stamped in big block letters.

"I didn't know if I should expect you today," Aggie said.

"Wouldn't miss it," Tessie answered. "Can we bring a horse for me to get back here?"

"I'll get Sunset," Nell said. "Want a saddle?"

Tessie shook her head, and Nell went to the pasture to bridle the mare. She tied her to the tailgate and rejoined Aggie on the seat.

Tessie moved next to Clara who rested on several blankets and who looked bigger than ever. She handed Clara a couple of newspapers she had brought along. Clara smiled in appreciation.

"How are you feeling?" Tessie asked.

"Getting ready for the big day," Clara replied breathlessly.

Tessie studied Clara closely. She looked a little

pinched around the mouth, and her eyes looked a little dull. Sick today? Or due at any moment? Lately, that thought had crossed Tessie's mind many times. Clara wasn't supposed to deliver for a couple more weeks. That's what she had calculated.

Tessie wondered if Clara actually knew when she got pregnant. Not eating properly, always on the road, always scared, wondering what the next day would bring, a woman could be pregnant and not suspect it for a month, maybe as long as two, the hard living keeping her thin and every day keeping her hungry and not paying attention to signs.

Clara could be ready right now. She had been feeling the baby kick harder and harder lately. Tessie always thought the baby had kicked awfully early for a November delivery. Clara could be dead wrong about that date.

"I want a girl," Nell said from the driver's seat.

"What do you want?" Tessie asked Clara.

"Oh, I don't care," Clara answered. "I just want a healthy kid. I already been thinking of names if it's a boy or a girl."

Tessie took Clara's hand in her own, ignoring the look that passed between Nell and Aggie. "Your kid'll be as strong as a horse, Clara. You're strong."

Clara rested against Tessie's side. "I been through a lot. Especially when I first got pregnant. I hope that didn't hurt me."

"Goodness, no," Aggie said. "Just think of all the women who've crossed this country in a covered wagon and had babies. They did just fine, and you will too."

"That's what my great-grandma did," Clara said. "Back in eighteen seventy-four. Her and Great-

162

Grandpa went by mule and wagon all the way from Ohio to Oregon. They couldn't afford to take a train. There was a depression on just like now, Great-Granny told me. She had my grandma on the way."

"You ought to write all that down, Clara," Nell said. "Nowadays people fly from city to city in no time at all. But then? Just imagine."

"Was a fellow, Fred Lockley, a newspaper man in Oregon, talked to Great-Grandma one time," Clara told her listeners. "Spent all afternoon with her and wrote down all she said. So it's on paper somewheres."

"My word, it tires me just to think of traveling all that way in nothing but a wagon," Tessie said.

"Me too," Clara replied.

Tessie thought Clara looked tired, all right, more tired than when they had first started for the fields not fifteen minutes ago. She put her arm around Clara. "Here, rest against me, for your great-grandmother's sake."

"Good idea, Tessie," Aggie said, laughing. "I'll bet her great-granny never had anyone put his arm around her while she was traveling by wagon across the plains."

"Or put *her* arm around her, like Tessie here is doing," Nell put in, causing Tessie to blush.

"Probably not," Clara agreed, leaning heavily against Tessie. "It feels good." She closed her eyes and dozed.

"What's the news in town this week, Tess?" Nell asked.

"The same."

"Always will be," Aggie said.

"I never did tell you two," Tessie said, "but I'm real pleased to see you back in church regular." A month ago, Nell and Aggie had come in by wagon just as services had begun. They walked inside wearing their prettiest dresses and hats, their heads held high, ignoring everybody they passed and the whispers they couldn't help but overhear. They boldly took seats right in the front pew. Aggie didn't play the organ, and Nell didn't sing in the choir — but they were there. And each Sunday they left right away not stopping to talk to anyone, and only barely receiving acknowledgments that they were even in the building. Tessie knew that coming to church was costing them, not only in terms of time lost in the fields but in what it must be doing to their hearts. She wondered if she could endure as much.

"Den of lions," Nell answered.

They arrived at the south field at seven. Tessie squinted at the pale blue sky speared by warm yellow rays from the sun. The star looked big on the horizon. It had been an exceptionally warm and dry fall with only occasional rains and none of them particularly heavy. If the weather remained steady, it would make it a thousand times easier for everyone to move potatoes to the train. Tessie hoped for the women's sake that their good luck would hold. Something ought to go right for them for a change.

Tessie laid blankets by a wagonwheel and made Clara as comfortable as possible. She fussed over her, tucking her coat tighter around her body and pulling her knit hat down low over her ears. "I want to be sure you stay warm, honey. Never mind how

164

that old sun up there is making you feel. I'll work the rows closer to you."

Clara did a quick intake of breath, her face screwed up in pain.

Alarmed, Tessie asked, "You okay, Clara?"

"Just a little crampy," Clara answered. "Was yesterday, too, but it passed. Too much breakfast this morning."

Tessie smiled, forcing herself not to look concerned. She kissed Clara on the cheek and grabbed a stack of baskets and a fork from the back of the wagon.

Each woman began at the end of a row. With the heel of her boot, she pushed the fork beneath the remains of a dead plant and tilted the tines upward, unearthing several well-formed, light-brown-skinned tubers. All were three to eight inches long.

After digging up a few more hills, Nell called across the rows, "It's a good crop this year."

Aggie nodded. "I bet I've got a three pounder here." She hefted a potato.

"Save that one for supper," Tessie said. She carefully put the potatoes into a basket. Later this afternoon, they would be bagged and loaded onto the wagon. If they had a chain link conveyor with the chains doing the work of digging beneath the tubers and forcing them to the surface, this field could have been harvested in the length of time it took three women digging by hand to complete five rows. If they had the sorter, they could load the crop onto the wagon in baskets and later this evening sort in the cellar at twice the speed. With neither convenience available, the potatoes would be brushed clean of as much dirt as possible, sorted and bagged on site. The bags would then be toted back to the cellar and stored there until shipping time.

Tessie stood and stretched her aching back muscles as she looked at the work still left to do. There was no possible way all this acreage would be harvested. No way at all. She cried inside at the devastating loss facing Nell and Aggie. They were so determined, yet sure to lose not only the crop but everything they owned because half these potatoes were destined to rot in the ground.

By the time each woman had dug her first two rows, she was ready to guzzle switchel. At the wagon, Tessie took her cup and a second one over to Clara and sat down beside her. "How are you doing, honey?"

"I feel awfully wet down there." She looked at the lap of her sundress.

"Good Lord, she's in labor!" Nell exclaimed.

"It's your water breaking!" Tessie said calmly. "I believe you're going to have a baby."

"I don't know nothing about having a baby. Lost the others after a few weeks." Clara sounded panicky. "Don't we need to boil gallons of water or something?"

Tessie answered, "Men are told to do that to give them something to do."

"I wish she could have seen a doctor at least once," Nell said.

"No time for talk now, girls," Tessie said lightly, not feeling light about anything at all. "Now honey, don't you worry about a thing. I've delivered children before. One when I was only fourteen years old and the last one only four years ago."

166

"Should I lay down?" Clara asked, and went into a hard contraction.

When it had passed, Tessie asked, "How long have you been feeling like this?"

Clara was limp. "Quite a while," she said breathlessly. "I didn't want to say anything."

"We need to time your contractions. Do you have any idea how far apart they are? And no, don't lay down. You'll feel worse."

"I don't know," Clara said. She was sweating hard and already gripped by another contraction.

"Breathe like a puppy," Tessie said. "It'll help you relax. Pant. Like this. Huh, huh, huh."

"Huh, huh, huh," breathed Clara. "Oh God, I hurt."

"Breathe, huh, huh, huh."

"Huh, huh, huh."

"Aggie, you hold Clara's hands," Tessie directed. "She'll squeeze tight."

"Only because I'm worried." Clara gasped, coming out of the cramp.

"Don't be," Tessie answered, helping Clara bend her knees. "Women have been doing this for some time now." Clara had long since stopped wearing panties. None in the Tucker/Abbott household fit. Several dresses had been let out, too.

Tessie asked, "Do either one of you have a knife?"

Nell fumbled in her pocket for hers.

Tessie pitched a pack of book matches at her. "Get a fire going and sterilize it. Give it to me when I say. For God's sake, don't touch the blade."

"I haven't got anything to boil water in," Nell answered in a nervous voice.

167

"Use the milk can lid," Aggie said. She jumped on the wagon and yanked the lid free of the can. Meanwhile, Nell had started to scour the ground for enough dead wood.

Clara began to moan. "Uhhhh, something's . . . something's happening."

Aggie lit a match beneath the small stack Nell had gathered. "How'd she get so far along and us not know?"

"I'd say over the years she's learned to bear a lot of pain," Tessie said, wiping Clara's brow, "and doesn't know when it's an ugly thing or when it's supposed to be reasonable and part of a natural, beautiful event. You're doing just fine, Clara. Your baby's trying to come out. Just rest and breathe like a puppy when you feel bad. It'll help ease the pain. Bend your knees a little more. Get ready to push when I tell you."

In fifteen minutes, Clara was pushing on Tessie's command and alternately grunting and relaxing. Sweat streamed down her face, forming a rivulet at her chin and soaking her dress. "I don't know how much more I can stand," she whispered.

Tessie massaged the insides of Clara's thighs. "You won't have to stand it much . . . Push, Clara, push!"

Clara pushed. She clutched Aggie's hands and screamed. Nell hovered over her, wiping the sweat from her face and neck while keeping a hand on Clara's shoulder to let her know she was there.

Clara's body convulsed and a tiny cry pierced the air.

"You're a momma, Clara," Tessie cried. "You're a momma!"

Clara collapsed, exhausted. She managed to gasp, "Let me see it. Is it all right?"

"Just a minute," Tessie said. "I need to cut the cord."

Deftly, she cut and tied the cord with sterilized thread from Clara's dress hem. With warm damp rags Nell had produced from her shirt tail, she wiped the baby clean, then wrapped the infant in her sweater before handing her to Clara. "You have a daughter, Clara. Six pounds, if she's an ounce." Tears blurred her vision.

Clara tenderly took her baby in her arms. "She's beautiful, just beautiful. Just look at that blonde hair." Again Nell wiped Clara's face, gently blotting away the tears that flowed down her cheeks.

Aggie assisted Tessie with Clara's afterbirth. When she had been tidied up, Aggie straightened Clara's dress and covered her with the others' coats. Tessie tucked herself tightly along Clara's side, supporting her as she had done on the wagon. "You're a momma, Clara honey. A momma!" Something Tessie would never be. She fought off tears in her painful longing for a child of her own.

"Do you have a name for her?" Nell whispered.

"I thought I would call her after my great-grandma Henrietta. Henrietta Tessie. Nettie for short."

"You would name her after me?" Tessie asked. She felt her heart swell.

"You're my friend ... I love you, Tessie."

"I love you, too, Clara. You and your baby are beautiful."

Clara's eyes took them all in. "Nettie's here because of you. Because of all of you."

"She's as welcome as her momma for as long as she wants to stay," Nell said.

Clara rested for an hour before her three nurses helped her and Nettie onto the wagonbed.

Nell chuckled. "What an excuse to stop digging potatoes."

The adults grinned and talked softly all the way home.

Nettie learned to nurse.

CHAPTER FIFTEEN

For days, Nell and Aggie took turns sweating and toiling alone in the fields, alternately working mornings and afternoons, not daring to leave Clara to care for herself and Nettie. The pregnancy and delivery had taken most of her strength.

"You shouldn't have to nurse me," she told them. "You have potatoes to dig."

"We can dig better with a half-day of rest in between," Aggie answered. "Now, you just get strong and nurse that baby. Eat and drink. Especially milk."

"I will," Clara promised.

But at night when they were alone in bed, Nell and Aggie fretted at their slow progress.

"We've got to work faster," Aggie said.

"Yeah? How?" Nell asked irritably.

"I don't know how," Aggie answered just as irritably. "We just have to, that's all."

And they did, driving themselves nonstop day after day. Once in a while Tessie came to help. She was only able to stay for a short time, but that time was a blessing, not because they could rest, but because they could harvest more.

"We should have forgotten about using Bibbs's tractor from the start," Aggie said one day. "We can't work this much land without a tractor to finish it for us. It was stupid of us to even try."

"I'd rather have used it to lose my crop just for the sake of having put one over on him," Nell said.

Aggie agreed.

One evening after Aggie had come in from the field, Nell said, "Tessie came visiting for about twenty minutes today. She held Clara's hand the whole time she was here. You don't suppose Tessie and Clara . . .?"

"Don't know, don't care," Aggie replied tiredly. She reached around and awkwardly rubbed her back with a thickly calloused hand. "I'm dying," she complained.

"You wish you were. Come on, let's go to bed. I'll rub your back for you."

"And I'll rub yours. You have to dig first tomorrow."

* * * * *

"Somebody's coming," Aggie said. She set down her coffee cup and walked to the door, squinting into the bright sunlight.

Nell and Clara joined her. "At six a.m.?" Nell asked. They walked out onto the front porch to await the car slowly making its way up the long drive.

Lucinda Epple pulled up before them; the car engine died.

Nell leaned close to Aggie. "Sending out church delegations kind of early, aren't they?"

Lucinda's bulk poured from the car. She was dressed in men's bib overalls.

"Either she's lost her mind," Aggie whispered back, "or she's lost her clothes. What's she doing here, dressed like that?"

Lucinda wheezed up to the porch, her eyes glaring, her jowls heavy on her cheekbones. "Tessie said a few days back you could use a hand." She loosened the scarf tied around her head.

Aggie looked distrustfully at her.

Lucinda balled a fist against a hip. "What about it? You two need help?"

Aggie felt her chest constrict. "Yes," she said. "We need help."

Lucinda put her hands in her pockets, then appearing uncomfortable with them there, pulled them out, daintily lacing her fingers together before her ample bosom. Dimples deeply shadowed her knuckles.

"How about coffee first?" Aggie offered. "We were just having some."

"Don't mind if I do," Lucinda said. "Heard about

the baby, too. Like to get a look at her. I got to go at noon," she clearly stated.

"At noon," Aggie agreed.

They finished their coffee quickly, Aggie awkward with Lucinda in her home. She felt like she was being studied by the big woman. Nell rose to get ready, and Lucinda rose with her.

"You go along too, Aggie," Clara insisted. "I feel really good this morning. I promise I'll rest a lot."

Aggie looked dubious.

"Go," Clara insisted. "It's been three weeks. I'm fine."

The labor that Lucinda produced was priceless. Most women and children helped in the fields at harvest time. Lucinda was proving that she had worked the land for years and that her size wasn't going to slow her down. She grunted and sweated, her shirt sticking to her skin as she turned hill after hill of potatoes, sorting and bagging and, with help, hauling them to the wagon.

Across a row, Nell whispered to Aggie, "If her heart explodes, we're in deep trouble."

Aggie wiped her brow with a bandanna. "It won't explode. You've heard her sing in choir. Lungs of a stud horse."

"That's lungs, not heart."

Lucinda didn't die of a heart attack, but when it was time for her to leave, she stuck the fork into the earth and said tiredly, "Take me back. I got to go."

She rode on the wagon box, her feet dangling off the end. Aggie sat defiantly beside Nell. Let Lucinda see them together. If she could make something of this, she was welcome to.

At the house, Aggie asked, "Can we offer you lunch, Lucinda? We ... can't pay you any money."

"Don't want your money, Aggie. Nobody has money — except for Bibbs."

Aggie wondered at the comment.

"Well, he's just been real fortunate over the years," Nell said charitably.

Lucinda looked like she wanted to say something. What are you thinking, Miss Lucinda, Aggie wondered, about Bibbs, about us?

"Got to go," Lucinda said abruptly. In two minutes, she was a cloud at the end of the driveway.

Aggie studied the settling dust. "I think she doesn't like us."

"I think she likes Bibbs less," Nell said.

"I can't believe she came to help us."

"Never look a gift horse in the mouth."

"Curiosity drove her out here."

"Maybe. Probably. She also came to help. Look how hard she worked. She didn't waste time looking for something to happen between us."

"Like this?" Aggie grabbed Nell and swung her around. With soft lips, she kissed her.

"My, my. Fifteen years down the line, and you still manage to curl my toes."

The quiet shuffle of receding feet just inside the kitchen door broke them apart.

They giggled as they went back inside to have a glass of lemonade before returning to the field.

Before they sat down, another car came up the lane. "Is Lucinda back?" Aggie asked.

"Not this time. Might be Tessie," Nell answered from the door.

"Tessie?" Clara flew to the porch, her baby carefully cradled in her arms. Her shoulders sagged in disappointment. "That's not her car."

"Hello in there!"

"My word," Aggie commented. "It's Emily Millington." The women gathered on the porch.

Emily bounced out of a Model A. She was dressed in a dark coat over a long skirt and workboots.

"Brought my fork." She held the tool out before them as if showing off a new toy.

Nell looked at Aggie. "What's going on?"

Emily was a short, pretty young woman to be married in the spring, rumor had it, to Willie Thomas. Her cheeks were rosy as apples, her hair black as pitch and her eyes as blue as the sky. She had sung in the choir until the gossip about Aggie and Nell had started. Then she had quit cold. Aggie assumed the gossip did it and wondered what made Emily come to work, which was obviously what she had come to do.

"Somebody in town said you could use a hand out here," Emily said. She smiled. Aggie thought of sunshine.

"You're the second one who's come today," Nell said.

"That so?" Emily answered. "Well, that's a blessing, isn't it? Got any water? I'm dry as a dust bowl."

"Water, switchel or lemonade?" Aggie offered.

"Switchel."

Again, the women labored, quitting just before the sun went down. Aggie insisted that Emily share

176

supper with them. Seated across from her, Aggie asked, "Won't someone be wondering where you are?"

Smiling widely, Emily replied, " 'Course he will. But I don't tell him everything. It makes him love me more if I'm a bit mysterious."

"What did you tell him, and I assume you mean Willie?" Aggie remarked.

"Said I was going to go off by myself to think about my wedding day — and night."

Clara guffawed loudly.

"My, a skeptic," Emily said.

"Her man ran out on her," Nell informed her.

Emily nodded. "I heard that. Mine runs out on me, I'll find him and shoot him."

"Good idea," Aggie said, laughing.

"A great idea," Clara agreed.

That night Aggie sat in the claw-footed, white porcelain tub in steaming hot water and suds up to her armpits, soaking away her aches and pains, while Nell, sitting naked on the tub's edge, scrubbed her back. "Even with Lucinda's and Emily's help today, we barely made a dent," Aggie said.

"Don't think about it," Nell answered. "We'll do what we can and let the rest go."

Aggie groaned. "I can't think about it. I can barely talk about it. I'm finished here. Let me up." She rinsed and quickly dried off, wrapping the towel around herself. "Get in. I'll wash your back."

She sudsed Nell thoroughly, then slid her hand over and around Nell's breasts. "You're as smooth as ivory."

"And you're as slick as an oilstick."

"I love to wash your body."

"Hmmm, you do it so well." Nell leaned against the tub's sloping back and gave herself up to Aggie.

Aggie dropped the cloth into the water. It disappeared in the suds. She let her towel fall to the floor and stepped into the tub, her feet between Nell's. She leaned forward, her hands on Nell's shoulders, her body rippling with muscles.

"My God, you're strong, woman," Nell whispered.

"Old, though."

"Doesn't matter. You're still strong . . . and good."

"Only good?"

"Great. You're great."

"I fell asleep the last time."

"I didn't say *I* was great."

Aggie squatted between Nell's knees. She let her fingers slide down Nell's neck, stopping at her nipples and circling them until they were hard. Awkwardly, she leaned forward taking one in her mouth.

"I'm sorry I fell asleep," Aggie said, slowly forming her words around Nell's nipple.

"Wasn't your fault."

"Wasn't yours either, darling. Don't talk." Aggie moved a hand to the inside of Nell's thighs.

"I'm getting a cramp in my back, Aggie."

Aggie released her. "Come on. Let's get out of here. I never did like making love in the tub. Reminds me of us making love in the back seat of a car."

"That brings back some memories." Nell rose, and Aggie rinsed her using a glass and clear warm water. "It wasn't comfortable then, and I doubt it'd be comfortable now."

They toweled each other dry, then Nell pulled

Aggie close, breathing softly in her ear. "This is torture. Let's get out of here."

They threw on their robes and moved to the bedroom, closing the door behind them.

Nell lay down, pulling Aggie with her. "I love you, strong woman."

"I love you, stronger woman."

Nell slid over Aggie. Her hand slipped between Aggie's thighs.

Aggie spread her legs, allowing Nell to touch her in her special place. She felt her flesh swell, felt herself become wet with heat.

Nell moved to Aggie's breasts, kissing them, tugging at her swollen nipples with demanding lips. She moved lower still, encircling Aggie's navel with her tongue, moving to her coarse hair. "You taste salty," she whispered.

Aggie smiled into the darkness. Nell always said that. It didn't matter that after fifteen years of sleeping with her, Nell was no longer very creative. It only mattered that Nell drove her wild each and every time they had ever made love — until the other night when Aggie had fallen asleep. She fought off the thought, afraid she would lose the warm sensations galloping up her inner thighs and colliding with her heart that was raging nearly out of control.

Nell's tongue pushed against her, stopped, pushed against her, stopped and drove itself inside her.

Aggie slipped her fingers through Nell's hair, pulling Nell's face against her, almost sitting now in an effort to take her further into her.

Sparks danced in front of her eyes as she arched, arched again and then collapsed, her energy seeping out of her. She heaved a long and deeply satisfied sigh.

After a long time, Nell released her, moving against her side. "You died, didn't you? I know you did."

"You are the greatest living thing on earth."

"You've said that before."

Aggie could feel Nell break into a grin.

"I have, haven't I?" Aggie murmured.

"You have."

"And what do you say every time?"

"I think it's something like: 'Ahhh, that's good, that's so good,' and then I think I tell you that I love you."

"You know you do, you old woman." Aggie could barely make her lips work.

"We've been together too long."

"You think so?"

"Hmmm."

"I need to find out." Aggie pulled herself upright and bit Nell gently on the neck.

"Don't be fooling with me."

Aggie regained her strength and her passion. She sat across Nell's thighs. "I won't fool, darling. I'll be perfectly serious." She locked Nell's legs shut with her own and slid an exploring finger into the tightness of Nell's lips.

"You know this is unbearable."

"I know," came a whisper. Aggie pushed Nell's lips apart just the tiniest bit. She smiled and used one hand to caress Nell's breasts, the other to touch her warm, moist flesh. She moved off Nell's legs and bent to kiss her.

Nell moaned as Aggie slowly opened Nell's thighs. She spread Nell's lips and touched her.

Nell drew her knees up tight against her chest and held her knees with her hands.

Aggie touched Nell once. In the darkened room, Aggie couldn't see Nell's face, but she knew that Nell's lips were drawn back against her gums, her eyes sealed against all life.

The throbbing that Aggie felt against her hand continued and continued and continued.

Finally, Aggie cradled herself between Nell's legs, her head resting on her lover's belly.

They fell asleep, repeatedly muttering to each other, "I love you, I love you."

CHAPTER SIXTEEN

"I don't get it," Nell said.

"Don't try to," Aggie answered as she worked alongside Nell, each digging potatoes, each sweating into the dirt in spite of the cool, overcast day. "Just be glad." She turned up seven hefty tubers.

"I don't like owing anybody," Nell replied. "Whether it's time, money or whatever."

"Thanks is all anyone has asked for, Nell. At least they're not spitting at us as they pass us."

"Not yet."

"Not at all. Now dig, damn it."

Several yards over, three women were harvesting while a fourth carefully put the potatoes into burlap bags before the four of them together, staggering under the weight of the bulky sacks, loaded them onto the wagon parked between the rows.

Since Lucinda and Emily had come, small groups of women had shown up daily. Today there were four; yesterday, three. They would all arrive in the same vehicle, bundled up in hats and coats and wearing heavy workboots, laughing and carrying on like they were going to a circus. They'd tramp onto the porch, chattering about F.D.R.'s New Deal, the minimum wage law passed by the Supreme Court on behalf of women, Joe Louis, Hitler, the Series and the Rose Bowl, the moving picture show — "Snow White and the Seven Dwarfs" — they'd seen in Boise, how Ginger was a better dancer than Fred because she had to dance backward all the time *and* in heels, and the latest Fibber McGee and Molly episode they'd heard on the radio. In the kitchen, they would make themselves at home over coffee and hold and help Clara diaper Nettie before following Nell and Aggie to the wagon to ride out to the northern fields that hadn't even been started before last week.

Clara talked right along with them, being the one person in the house who, through Tessie's papers, kept up on the news. Nell and Aggie were impressed that so many women were interested in something other than homes, husbands and children.

"They never mention world events at the Rock Wren," Tessie said one day when Aggie asked her about it. "But get them away from their men, and they show off their brains. I'm convinced we'd have less trouble in the world if we had a woman president."

Aggie scoffed, but Nell and Clara agreed.

Nell scrubbed away a thankful tear and pushed her boot against the fork. If the women continued to come, by mid-November they *would* get the potatoes dug! Not just most of them, but *all* of them.

Terrible way to do business, Nell thought, digging potatoes by hand. Another tuber surfaced. Backbreaking work. And for what? A piece of land? Yes, by damn, a piece of land. *Her* land. Hers and Aggie's. By God, they'd sell this crop and buy back everything they'd given up. They'd pay Clara and the mortgage on time every month. And they'd sit in the living room all winter long counting their profits. The crop was that good, that plentiful.

Nell's heart soared as she took just a moment to gaze at the working women, their coats open, wool hats or scarves thrust back on their heads, backs bent, their musical laughter floating across the rows, jokes and teasing being tossed around like pollen on a spring wind. Somebody was whistling, "Whistle While You Work." A couple more joined her.

The scene looked ideal, the volunteers lighthearted and chatty. Yet they never included Nell or Aggie in their bantering. They were respectful and listened to directions, going right to work and never slowing except to drink and eat lunch. But Nell always felt an unbearable wall between herself and them.

At least she and Aggie were respected. Not for

the way they lived — hell no, that would never happen — but by the way they worked. This must have been what Lucinda saw in them and told others — their willingness to kill themselves for this crop. Nell *would* kill herself for it, too. It was too good a year not to. And if Aggie's and her work habits kept the ladies coming, then she'd continue to kill herself just to show them, to convince them that she meant to stay in Grassy Flats in spite of any barbed wire or gossip or the town's banding together to drive them out.

She frowned, rethinking. When had she started saying "I mean to stay in Grassy Flats?" Had the thought somehow slipped in, that in spite of their hard-fought efforts, she and Aggie might lose everything after all? No, it couldn't happen. She wouldn't *let* it happen. She jabbed her fork into the soil.

"Nell, what's the matter with you?" Aggie had fallen several yards behind her. "You've been working like you hate these potatoes. Take it easy. We need every one."

"Sorry," Nell said. She slowed her pace, noticing an ache in her hands and arms.

She wondered what the ladies were telling their kin before coming out here, each with her own fork in hand. Tessie would know. She knew everything going on in town. It was good to have a friend like her working in the Rock Wren.

Suddenly, Nell was sick of thinking and of trying to out-think what everyone else was thinking. "Break!" she yelled. She had to get a drink. All this pondering was going to kill her before the digging ever did. She drove her fork deep into the ground and left it there.

The women stopped at her call and trooped over to the wagon. They threw down oilcloths and blankets and sank to the earth. They munched sandwiches, pickles and cookies and drank Thermoses of hot, steaming coffee each had brought along. They leaned heavily against wagon wheels, recovering their strength.

"Lord, I'm tired," Miranda Smith, the youngest of the group, said. "Lift that bar, tote that bale." She wiped her brow with the apron she wore over her coat.

"Oh, be still," Alma Bingham answered. "You never lifted a bar or toted a bale in your life." Alma Bingham had never been afraid to voice an opinion. She was big and boisterous and often intimidated newcomers to town.

Lura Hess, usually Grassy Flats's best-dressed lady, but today wearing mens' pants and boots and what looked like her husband's barn coat, took a sip of coffee, then muttered, "Probably doesn't even know what a bar is."

"I do too," Miranda countered. "It's a railing on top of a corral."

"Good Lord, girls, relax while you can. We've got work to do, and we shouldn't be wasting our energy bickering. Besides it's tote that barge and lift that bale." Iva Oakerman, the oldest of the group and nearing sixty was therefore the most respected. She brushed away slips of wayward hair that escaped from the snow-white braids wound around her head. "I've never known you girls not to argue, whether it's sitting on quilting committees or cleaning the church. Now, be still."

Nell hopped off the end of the tailgate where she and Aggie were eating. Nervously, she squatted down in front of the group. Almost in a whisper she asked, "Why are you ladies helping us? Why do you take the time? I know you have other important things to do. Maybe even work in your own fields."

"Lucinda said you needed help, and we can give up some time for you," Iva replied. The others nodded in agreement.

"That's all? No other reason?"

"What other reason could there be?" Miranda asked, looking too innocent.

"I'm not any different now than I've ever been," Nell told them, thinking she knew *exactly* the reason they were all here. Inquisitiveness!

"You're thinner, maybe," Iva said. "You too, Aggie. You folks always did work hard."

Nell removed her hat. No one was going to give her an honest answer. "When's the train due exactly?" she asked. It was tough being without a telephone or a truck. It cut down considerably on hearing the latest in town. She hadn't even seen a paper since the last time Tessie was out three days ago.

"Tomorrow," Iva said.

"*Tomorrow?*" Nell glanced at Aggie who looked like she'd just been kicked in the stomach.

"So soon?" Aggie asked.

"It ain't soon," Miranda said. "You all are just out of touch lately."

Nell stood. "Whose fault is that?" Anger flared in

her belly. There was no possible way to harvest the last two fields *and* get all they had bagged to the depot, *if* they could get all they had bagged there.

"Come on, girls," Iva spoke sharply. "Time to dig."

"Already?" Miranda said. She rose slowly, arching her back.

Alma grabbed her hand and helped her to her feet. "Come on, girl, you can do it."

"You sound like you're training a dog, Alma," Miranda replied. But she got to her feet.

The women headed back to their rows while Iva walked with Nell and Aggie. "I'm sorry about the way things are going for you girls," she said. "It isn't right what this town done to you. Of course, it isn't right what you two do to each other, but ..."

Aggie whirled on her, speaking in a low tone. "Don't make judgments, Iva, or you can take your ass and git. I don't need anybody's help that bad."

Iva coldly eyed her as Nell jammed her hands into her pockets to keep from smashing Iva's face. Shaking her head in apparent dismay, Aggie walked alone to the field.

"You hurt her, Iva," Nell accused. "You hurt me, too. Why'd you do that?"

Iva stopped and said, "I thought about you two a long, long time after I heard ..."

"Heard what?" Nell demanded.

"... that you and Aggie ... live like man and wife. It's just always bothered me."

Nell felt her face turn red. It shouldn't have. She had known what Iva was going to say.

"Is it true?" Iva asked.

It wouldn't matter what Nell told Iva. She would

still believe what she wanted to believe. Nell carefully answered, "Not being a man, I wouldn't know."

"That's no answer."

"I'm going to dig potatoes, Iva, not stand here and philosophize with you all day." Iva had gotten all the information she was going to get. Nell thought it was too darn much already.

Together, the women managed to harvest the entire field by sundown. Tonight, there would be extra grain for the horses. The animals would be working all night, hauling 2,400 pounds of potatoes per trip to the train depot.

A sinking depression engulfed Nell as she checked her watch. "Come on, ladies," she called out. "You've had enough."

They had. They stumbled over the rough ground, dragging their forks behind them. "Now I know what lift that bar and tote that bale *really* means," Miranda said.

"You're full of mule dust," Alma answered. "Get on that wagon."

On the way back, Iva asked across the bagged crop stacked in the wagonbox, "How're you going to get all your spuds to town before the train leaves, Aggie?" The women crowded together at the end of the wagon where a space had been left for them and the tools. No one was foolish enough to sit on the potatoes and possibly bruise them.

"I have no idea," Aggie answered from her seat beside Nell, where she had boldly ridden each day.

Nell said, "We're going to lose a lot this year. We had a bumper crop."

"Everybody had a bumper crop," Alma told them.

"Well, we did our best," Aggie said. "You helped. We'll be able to pay our mortgage at least."

"You going to buy back your piano, Aggie?" Lura asked.

Nell's face flamed. "How'd you know about that, Lura?"

"Lura Hess, you got the biggest mouth in Idaho," Iva scolded.

"It doesn't matter, Iva," Aggie said. "I'm sure all of Grassy Flats knows what we sold and when and how much we got for it. Probably Jeff Myers spread it all over town for anybody who missed seeing us hauling it in by wagon."

Lura said, "I only asked because I hope you get your piano back. You . . ." Lura paused. "Oh heck, Aggie, you have a talent. You ought to have your piano back. And you ought to be directing the church choir when you ain't workin' like a dog. Not just sitting up front looking like you're going to bite off the preacher's head."

"That's right, Aggie," Miranda agreed.

"I think so, too," Alma said. "So does Iva. She said so on the way out here how Aggie ought to get her piano back and be directing."

"So I did," Iva admitted.

"And their china. You said about that, too," Miranda reminded her.

"That was Alma," Iva corrected.

"I did not," Alma retorted. "I hoped they could get their truck back."

Nell was glad that dusk had fallen. They wouldn't see the tears in her eyes. She glanced at

Aggie's glistening eyes. Nell didn't think it was because of the small amount of dust that was rising from the horses' hooves.

Aggie brushed at her eyes and turned to face them. "I don't know about getting everything back. I doubt we'll be able to do that, after all. If we could get all our potatoes to the train, but now ... it doesn't look so good."

"You need a truck, Aggie," Miranda said.

"You need a conveyor, too. You can't be harvesting like this every year."

"You're not kidding," Lura heartily agreed.

Alma gave her a push. "Nobody forced you to come out here, Lura."

"I still don't know why you helped," Nell said, "why you're all helping. Iva said she was told we needed help. There's more, I think."

"Well, I'm going to tell," Miranda announced.

"Miranda," Iva warned.

"It's not fair," Miranda said. "They have a right to know."

Nell held her breath. She didn't want to hear repeated what Iva had told her earlier this afternoon, just the rest of it, if there was any more.

"The truth is," Miranda began, "what Bibbs did to you is awful. Just awful. To cut off somebody's water like that. It's not right. And you with an expectant lady in the house. No man should be able to do that to a woman with child, and that includes our men. It's criminal!"

"And," Lura said, "as long as we're telling it, I'd like to mention that we're just a little sick of our menfolks telling us every little thing we can or can't do. We want to do what we want to do from time to time, just like you two do."

"I think that's wonderful," Aggie replied. "You should be able to do that. But does anybody know why Bibbs blocked us off? We're no threat to him. He doesn't even work the land next to ours."

Nell tugged at Aggie's shirt sleeve. "Aggie, drop it."

"It's because he hates women," Iva said.

"Hates women?" Aggie echoed.

"Hates me mostly," Iva replied.

Nell's eyebrows went up a couple of notches. "Why you?"

"I refused his proposal years ago," Iva answered.

"You're kidding!" Lura exclaimed.

"Be still, Lura," Alma told her.

Iva said, "He never forgave me. Never forgave any woman."

"Isn't that kind of small-minded?" Nell asked. "There are other women."

"He didn't think so."

Miranda cleared her throat. "And when he learned about you two . . . not even seeming to need a man for anything, anything at all, well, he just . . ."

"Miranda," Iva warned.

"Well, it's true," Lura agreed. "I don't see anything wrong. I've never seen anything wrong. It's just rumors. Tell me, Aggie. Tell me, Nell. Tell us it's just rumors."

Nell swung around and in the dying light, looked at Lura, looked at them all, each in turn, knowing what they wanted to hear, what they *needed* to hear, what they could accept.

She felt a slithering thing slide up her belly and across her tongue and out her mouth. The thing, bitter and huge, snapped at her soul and crushed her insides. She said, "No, Lura, it's not true." She wanted to lay down and die.

"See? A drunk telling lies," Miranda said. "I saw Chester that day. He was drunk as a skunk, and we were all stupid enough to listen to him. I'm sorry, Nell, Aggie."

"We're all sorry," Alma added.

"Well, that's a relief," Iva said. "I told Gil it was just an ugly rumor. Just an ugly rumor and nothing else. That old Chester Olmstead. I never did like him much, him and his big mouth. Don't even like the way he looks. And his wife can't cook a lick, either. But mind you, if I saw one thing, *one* thing improper out here, I'd be gone in a flash."

"That's what I told Daniel," Lura said. "He didn't really want me to come, but I did anyway."

Alma laughed aloud. "My man bellowed up a storm. I finally told him I was going to visit Iva. Isn't that funny?"

Nell didn't think it was funny at all, and the way Aggie now sat so still and quiet on the seat beside her, she didn't think Aggie thought so either.

At the house, goodnights were quickly said.

Nell and Aggie stood arm in arm staring at the horizon's dying sunset.

"You think they believed you?" Aggie asked.

"I don't know. Some did. Some didn't. Doesn't matter."

"Then why do I have this searing pain in my chest called hurt?"

Nell put her arm around Aggie's waist. "Comes with loving me."

"No, it comes with not being allowed to love you — openly!"

CHAPTER SEVENTEEN

In the barn by the light of several lanterns and while the cats twined in and out of everybody's legs, Aggie and Tessie were busily slipping two-by-fours into brackets spaced around the perimeter of the wagonbox and bolting crossboards to them to keep the fully loaded wagon from dumping its cargo on the way to town tonight. Nell efficiently harnessed the six-horse team. Clara handed out whatever tool or strap was asked for.

"What'd you tell Dusty, Tess?" Nell asked. "How's he feel about you coming here at night?"

Dusty would be mad enough to slap her again that she came after dark, as if Nell or Aggie might grab her or something. She answered, "He doesn't know. He's miles on the other side of town. Edna Vogel's husband picked him up about six. It's their poker night. I doubt he'll be home before four or five in the morning. I don't know how he can get up and work all day long after only two hours of sleep. But he plays cards every Thursday night regular as clockwork. Has for years. Makes him damn mean, too, every Friday morning. Something else I can count on like clockwork."

She hadn't come before on Dusty's card nights, not wanting to become too much of a pest here. Lord knew she showed up often enough through the week.

But tonight she *needed* to see Clara just to see her. Clara seemed mighty glad to see her, too. Otherwise, she wouldn't have run up and hugged her so fast — and for so long, would she? She'd never done *that* before. It darn near scared Tessie to death — and thrilled her to her toes.

Aggie grunted as she tightened another bolt. "Come on, folks. Let's hurry and finish up. I want to grab a bite to eat before we leave."

Clara pulled off her work gloves. "I'll feed Nettie and make up a batch of sandwiches. Tomato do?"

Everybody allowed that it would.

Setting aside her wrench, Tessie added, "I'll give you a hand, Clara. Besides, you should rest for awhile. You've been going at it pretty hard out here."

In the kitchen, Tessie quickly prepared food and hot coffee, sending Clara off to nurse Nettie in the living room where, since Nettie's birth, her bed had been moved.

By the time Tessie came in, Clara had made herself comfortable, her back resting against a pillow, a patchwork quilt tossed across her legs and a lighted lantern on a nearby box. She had unbuttoned her sweater and dress and freed a plump breast. Nettie, wrapped in a thick, warm blanket, fed with obvious contentment, made tiny cooing noises. Clara hummed a tune Tessie recognized from childhood. She sat on the edge of the bed beside them.

Tessie had often watched Clara nursing. Dusty liked to do this to her. She wondered why it was that boys and men could perform this act all their lives, but women were limited to infancy. She thought she would like to try it and didn't *care* that she was a woman.

"I'm sure glad my milk's good," Clara remarked. "I'd just as soon keep Nettie off bottles as long as I can." She pulled the infant's tiny hat lower over her thick, yellow hair.

"I'll never have such a chance," Tessie said, her voice full of regret.

Clara sadly looked at Tessie. "I'm sorry, Tess."

They fell quiet while Nettie sucked noisily.

"Maybe," Clara said, "we could pretend you're feeding her. If you sat behind me . . ."

Tessie thought about that a moment. "I don't know . . ."

"Oh come on, Tess, be a sport," Clara encouraged. "Climb behind me. I'll sit between your legs." She moved forward to make room.

Tessie's blood roared in her ears as she pulled off

her work shoes, then positioned herself behind Clara who adjusted her back against Tessie's chest. "Now put your arms around me and take Nettie. I'll move my arms away. Got her?"

Tessie did, Nettie paying little attention to the activities involving her.

Tessie felt Nettie's full weight settle in her arms, felt the pressure of Clara's body pressing heavily against her, her warm, naked breast touching her arm. She felt Nettie's nursing motions jar her tiny body. She closed her eyes and rested her forehead against Clara's shoulder. A peace she'd never known before stole softly into her.

"Nettie's strong," Clara said contentedly. She relaxed even more, and Tessie wanted to crush woman and child to her and hold them there for all time.

She was breathing too loudly and too rapidly, certainly too close to Clara's ear. She turned her head away and pretended to study the lantern's steady light, conscious only of the messages being sent to her heart. She felt lightheaded, the way she had the very first time she met Clara.

Nettie fell asleep at Clara's breast, and Tessie let mother and baby go. There was a little popping noise as Clara pulled Nettie free of her nipple.

Tessie smiled and bit back tears. She removed herself and again sat on the edge of the bed and tugged on her boots.

Clara burped Nettie and changed her diaper. Tessie held the baby for a moment and kissed her good night before Clara laid her down in the rocker beside the bed. Clara again sat back against the pillows and threw the quilt over her legs.

Tessie watched lights from the lamp dance in Clara's eyes. "Thank you, Clara, for sharing yourself and your child with me."

Shyly, Clara replied, "It wasn't anything."

"Oh, yes it was, Clara. It was a lovely gift."

"Well . . ."

Clara's lips looked so soft. Tessie wondered if they would be that soft if she touched them. As Clara gazed at her, they curved into a gentle smile.

Tessie suspected Clara would be as interesting to kiss as Nell had been in her dream. She blinked rapidly and looked away, thinking she would like to find out, thinking she couldn't leave this room *until* she found out. She knew with a certainty if she couldn't get past this moment, she didn't have a future.

She clutched her shaking hands in her lap, no longer able to look into Clara's eyes. Her voice trembled slightly as she quietly said, "I'd like to ask you something, Clara. And if you say no, I'd like you to promise you'll never tell what I asked."

"My goodness, Tessie. What could be that secretive?"

Now Tessie looked at her. "Promise first."

Clara continued that easy smile. "All right. I promise."

"For sure?"

"For sure, Tessie. You've been real good to me. Wonderful. I think about that a lot. So . . . I promise." She patted Tessie's arm.

Tessie unlocked her hands and moved the lantern to the floor, plunging them into soft shadows. She breathed deeply, her heart already hurting, anticipating Clara's refusal — and laughter. "Would you mind ..." She cleared her throat, stalling. Ask her! her mind screamed. "Would you mind if I ... kissed you?"

Clara looked surprised. "Kissed me?"

"Yes, you know ... on the lips."

"Lips?"

"Like ... like your husband ... might."

"He wasn't much of a kisser, Tessie. I didn't really like it."

"Would you let me?"

Clara shrugged in confusion. "I don't know. To kiss a lady on the lips seems ... strange."

"Aggie and Nell do. I know they do ... all the time."

"You've seen them?"

"No, but I still know they do. They ... love each other ... like husbands and wives do."

"Well," Clara mused, "I never knew two women who paid attention to each other the way they do. Anyway, I saw them once."

"It's a big secret with them. But they're real happy, you know. So ... may I?"

"My teeth ... they ... don't look so good." Clara put a hand to her lips, and Tessie gently moved it aside.

"They don't look that bad. Besides, never mind them. We'll get you new teeth. May I?"

"New teeth? How are we going to ...?"

"May I?"

Clara fell silent, not saying yes, but not saying no, and Tessie leaned forward, tentatively pressing her lips against Clara's. She lingered there, parting her lips slightly and felt her heartbeat soar. The kiss was far more beautiful than her dream.

Then Clara pulled away and smiled. "That wasn't so bad after all, Tessie." She put her hands to her face as if to hide reddened cheeks. "It was better than Hank's sloppy, wet kisses."

Tessie felt her own face heat up. "It was better than Dusty's, too."

"Almost makes me wonder if other women know about this kind of kissing."

"They know," Tessie said. "They just don't believe in it. Not between two women, anyway. Or, those who do believe in it, like Nell and Aggie, just don't talk about it." Hesitantly, she leaned toward Clara again.

Clara pulled back slightly and Tessie froze. Had this single kiss been it? The only one Clara would ever give her? She thought she would die if it was.

After an eternity, Clara put her hand on Tessie's shoulder, tugging slightly, calling Tessie to her with her fingertips. Tessie moved against her, and they kissed a second time. Clara seemed more relaxed, more involved. They kissed softly, Tessie barely daring to move her lips until she felt Clara's teeth against her own. Awkwardly, their arms encircled each other.

Tessie suddenly felt out of control as heat piled up in her belly. Unexpectedly, Clara tightened her arms hard against her. Their mouths pressed painfully together, the closeness of their bodies crushing each other sending powerful shockwaves through Tessie's mind and pure desire throughout her body.

They broke apart.

"Lord, Clara!" Tessie would have backed away to catch her breath, but Clara held her firm.

Unsteadily, Clara whispered, "It ... was nice ... wasn't it?"

"Yes ... yes ... it was very nice," Tessie managed to whisper.

Then Clara released her.

Anxiously, Tessie spoke. "I can't stay. I can't even *stay!*" She glanced around feeling a little panicky. She wanted to remain here, to never, ever leave.

Clara stroked Tessie's hair and face. "You can come back. You *have* to come back. I ... need you, and you ... have to feed Nettie."

Tessie clutched Clara's shoulders. "I'll come back. I *swear* I'll come back."

"Clara!" Nell's voice calling from the kitchen yanked Tessie off the bed and onto her feet.

"In here," Tessie answered too loudly. She was aware of how shaky her voice sounded.

"Food ready? We've got to get going. I'm going after Aggie."

"Be right there!"

As soon as Tessie heard the front door close, she sat back down and grabbed Clara's hands in both her own. "Listen, honey," she said. "I ... I have a secret."

"Another secret?"

"Almost as big as the last one," Tessie said. "I never told anyone. Not even Dusty. I want to tell you."

"Why?"

"Because I ... think we can do something with it — if it's true. We can begin a new life, even get new teeth for you."

Clara looked puzzled. "Your husband wouldn't want another woman in his house."

"I'm not talking about *his* house. I'm talking about *our* house. I'm talking about leaving Dusty and living with you."

"You're joking!"

"I'm not." Tessie looked furtively around. "This secret . . ." She glanced around again.

"They're out to the barn," Clara said.

"I don't trust anybody. Not even Nell and Aggie." She jumped up and looked out the window. By their lanterns, she could see their shadowy figures standing by the barn door. She had the feeling they were giving her and Clara time. She hurried back to Clara's side and continued. "My father made me promise not to tell anybody except my husband."

"I'm not your husband, Tessie."

"Nature's oversight." Tessie's voice dropped low. "I've got a box hidden away. It used to be Pa's. He knew a couple of fellows, Zack Meadows and Dan Slates. He joined up with them for a while. Years ago after Ma died he went a little crazy, did some stupid things, outlaw things. He gave the box to me when he was dying."

"What's in it?" Clara whispered, now apparently caught up in Tessie's mood.

"A piece of oilcloth, a map that tells where those men hid money. Lots of it, Pa said."

"Why wouldn't the other men have taken the money by now?"

"The law shot Meadows and Slates trying to escape. Pa served time. When he got out, he dug up the map where they'd buried it when they were all running. He never dared go after the money, he said. He figured they were still watching him."

"And not his daughter?"

203

"No lawman's ever come near me other than our sheriff, and he only comes into the diner for coffee. He's never asked me a question. Not one. But don't think I haven't worried about it from time to time." She grabbed Clara's shoulders. "Honey, all we have to do is be at the lava beds next year on June twenty-first, stand where the map says and hope like hell the sun is shining because at high noon it casts a shadow right on the spot where the money is. It says so right on the map."

Clara looked incredulous. "You're dreaming. I've been by those beds. They could slash you to ribbons walking across them."

A million years ago, volcanic peaks spewed forth molten rock that flowed over the earth, covering it as far as the eye could see. Left was a hostile, uneven, rust-colored terrain with nothing to offer but a sun that could bake hatless brains to death and lava that could make mincemeat out of flesh.

"I'm not dreaming, Clara, and we're going to find it — together! We can borrow or steal what we need to do it. Clara ..." Tessie clutched Clara to her breast. "You gotta have hope, honey. My Pa gave me that map. He wouldn't lie to me. Not when he was dying. Please, try with me. Say you will. I've been thinking about this for years and years. Never knew how I could do it alone. With you, I could. Come with me. Don't tell me life has killed all your dreams."

"Would you turn in the money if you found it?"

"Are you kidding? Anyway, who knows who Pa took it from? It happened a long time ago."

"But Dusty ..."

"Nuts to Dusty. We're going alone. Please, Clara."

"And Nettie?"

"She comes. She's like my own. I loved her before she was born. I laid my head on your belly and listened to her sounds and felt her kick. I delivered her. Tonight, I fed her. She's a part of me too."

There was an intense look in Clara's eyes. "All right, Tess. We'll leave Nettie with my ma for a while and go. June twenty-first is a long ways away. But I'll be there with you. It'll be a nice vacation."

"I'm not talking about a vacation, Clara. I had something longer in mind. I'd ... I'd just as soon you stay with me and me with you, if you don't mind. I've thought about it from time to time, and ..."

Clara's eyes filled with tears. "You're not kidding about this house thing, are you?"

Tessie brushed the tears away. "I don't know where other than the lava beds we'd head, Clara, but it wouldn't be Grassy Flats. And I'd like to head there with you. We'd probably have to rent a horse and wagon. And I got a little money stashed in my box. Dusty's out of my life as soon as I can take care of things. Just give me some time to get it worked out a little. It won't take me long."

"He'll kill you."

"He hasn't got the guts. Next time I walk into this house, we could be together all the time."

"I'd like that," Clara answered. "All the time."

Tessie couldn't tear her eyes away from Clara's. She was not at all herself, not the *new* self she was feeling. "I think I'd like to say I love you, Clara. I think I'd like to say I love you very much."

Clara kissed the palms of Tessie's hands, first one, then the other. "I think I would like to say that I love you too, Tessie."

They held each other once more, kissing deeply.

This time, they both hopped off the bed when Nell called from the kitchen.

CHAPTER EIGHTEEN

"What do I hear?" Nell put down the sandwich she had been gulping, walked to the kitchen door and pulled aside the curtain. "That's some string of cars coming down the road."

Aggie had gotten up, too. "Never saw so many out here at one time. Especially on a weeknight. Wonder where they're all going.

The first set of lights turned into the drive. "Somebody's coming up here," Nell said.

Clara pushed back her dress sleeves. "If it's that no good man of mine . . ."

"Relax, Clara," Tessie said. "He wouldn't dare."

"Good Lord, they're all coming here," Aggie exclaimed. One after another, the other vehicles followed at a high rate of speed.

"Get the gun, Aggie." Nell spoke with perfect control while her innards began to shake and her knees weaken.

"Is there a Ku Klux Klan anywhere near here?" Clara anxiously asked. She moved closer to Tessie who stood back from the door.

"Never heard of any," Tessie replied just as anxiously. "Maybe our men are so angry at us for helping you, they're going to drop by and have a talk about it, but I bet they don't talk."

"Well, we can stand here and wonder, or we can go out there and face them, whoever they are," Nell said. "I'm for showing them who *I* am."

Aggie was the one who opened the door. "We've faced others on this porch this year. Let them come." She stepped out into the night; the others followed.

Seven cars and eight pickups roared to a dusty stop.

Alma Bingham, first in line, got out of her husband's truck. Other women piled out of their vehicles. Nell breathed a big sigh of relief. "Alma, you scared the living daylights out of us. What are you doing here?" The same women who had worked earlier today were also back. So was Lucinda and a dozen other women she knew, dressed in warm coats and pants and wool hats and scarves and boots. "What are *all* of you doing here?"

"No way to call you people and let you know we were coming," Iva answered for them all. "Hope we didn't scare you."

"Come on, gals," Alma directed. "Back to your cars. The fields are this way."

"Hold it. *Hold* it!" Aggie yelled. "Will somebody tell us what's going on?"

"We're here to help you harvest those last two fields," Alma pronounced. "There's no man got a right to do you the way our men have. We've come to make up for it."

Nell, remembering she still held the gun, put it aside and held up her hands in protest. "I appreciate this, ladies, but I'm not going to let you do it. Your men'll be as mad at you as they are at Aggie and me."

Miss Laura Million Turnstall, a tiny woman who didn't stand five feet high, had been sitting in Alma's truck. Two women helped her from the cab. A cane in each hand, she moved unassisted through the group. They parted like the Red Sea. Miss Turnstall looked to be a hundred years old, she herself said she wasn't sure, and was seen out of her house exactly once a year for Christmas Eve services. Nell gawked at her presence, slammed her mouth shut and, with the others, remained respectfully quiet. The old woman tottered up, blanketed in a thick coat and heavy scarf.

"Welcome to my home, Miss Turnstall," Nell said. Aggie quickly put the porch rocker beside the ancient woman.

Miss Turnstall nodded her thanks as she sat. Nell knelt beside her. She had to shout to make the woman hear her. "You shouldn't have come out tonight, Miss Turnstall. It's chilly."

Miss Turnstall's voice crackled like static electricity. "It'd be a lot chillier if it was men and not ladies here tonight." The skin on her face looked papery, and her eyes watered in the cool air. "Now you listen to me, young lady."

Nell listened. They all listened.

"This town gets mean 'bout once a year. Always has."

Nell didn't think it was that often, but she knew it could get mean.

"Grassy Flats is just looking for a reason to get rid of two girls who don't need anybody. Especially men! I been without a man all my life, not that there ain't been beaus, mind you. None of 'em reached my standards. Smokers and drinkers, all. But they think a woman can't do without 'em. That's all this whole mess has been about. Ain't that true, ladies?" She turned, glaring at them. "Well, ain't it? Alma, you rode me out here. Sitting right next to me you told me how you admired these ladies' independence. Didn't you tell me that?"

"I did tell you that," Alma answered.

"It's all against the Bible," Miss Turnstall said, jabbing her finger into the air.

What is? Nell wondered. Cutting off their water? Being forced into selling personal possessions? Kissing another woman? Which one?

"So we're out to show him . . ." someone said.

"Who?" Aggie asked.

"Harry Bibbs," said another.

"Or Jeff Myers and his damn bank for . . ."

"Or any like them . . ."

". . . including our husbands," someone insisted.

". . . that he can't do this to people. Who knows who might be next?"

"It's against the Bible for men to do women thataway," Miss Turnstall said.

Now Nell understood. "Only if you displease Mr. Bibbs, Miss Turnstall," Nell said. "Or Mr. Myers."

A vehicle came down the road. Nell stood and watched it approach. It reached the driveway, then passed by, its red taillights fading into the night. Thank God it wasn't some irate husband. "Listen to me, ladies," she said. "The men you talk about are your husbands. They'll give you what for when you get back. Go on home now, and stay out of our troubles. We thank you for the help you've given and the help you're offering, but I don't want you making anyone angry. Now go, please, before your men come after you."

Aggie, who until now had remained silent, said sharply, "Oh, shut up, Nell. They want to help. We need the help, and I'm for it." She snatched up a fork leaning against the porch. "Come on, Alma. You drive. I'll get a lantern and grab my coat."

Iva stepped close to Nell. "We thought you'd be the stubborn one, Nell. We also thought you'd listen to Miss Turnstall if you would listen to anyone."

"I don't even know her."

"She's smart. You know that much about her. Nobody gets to be a hundred without learning something about people. Even closed up in that house of hers like she is, she knows that what's going on in Grassy Flats is wrong, and it needs to be made right. Well?" Iva stood rigid, her arms crossed in front of her.

For once in her life, Nell followed Aggie without comment, deeply worried about everyone.

Iva and Miss Turnstall returned to Grassy Flats. The rest, including Tessie, who took the time to tuck in Clara, caravaned to the fields. They were led by Aggie and Nell who rode with Alma.

"How did the ladies manage to get their husbands' vehicles?" Nell asked. "And where're their children?"

Alma grunted as the truck struck a hole. "Everybody said they were going to EmmyLou's house to help with her delivery. The children have been put up with those who couldn't make it and whose husbands are out playing poker tonight."

Aggie pulled her wool hat lower over her ears. "I heard EmmyLou wasn't due till next month. Is she delivering tonight?"

"No," Alma replied, "but men usually don't question things like that. If we tell them she's about to deliver, they believe us."

"What if somebody calls wanting to speak to his wife?" Nell asked.

Alma carefully steered around a small rock. "Iva's going over there for that. She'll tell him his wife can't come to the phone right now."

"But this job may take all night," Nell said.

"Sometimes so does delivering a baby," Alma answered.

"Covered it all, didn't you?"

"Like to think we did."

The truck hit another hole. The riders quickly put their hands on the dash to steady themselves while Alma tightly clutched the wheel. "Damn," she said. "I come back with a busted axle, and I *will* be in hot water."

They reached the fields a short time later. With

lighted lanterns, they gathered as a group to await instructions.

"It's a big field," Nell said. "We planted like fools."

"A tractor does help, doesn't it?" Emily Millington said.

There was light laughter, easing Nell's mind. "Wouldn't know," she answered. "Don't own one and couldn't rent one."

More laughter followed, and Nell continued, "Work in teams of four, three digging and one filling a bag. Forget the culls. We'll get them later." Any further directions were unnecessary. These folks had been working in the fields for years.

"Let's do it!" Tessie cried enthusiastically. She was grinning from ear to ear.

"What's struck you?" Alma asked.

"Oh, nothing," Tessie said. "I just want to get this job done and get on with my life."

Disbelievingly, Ramona asked, "Working in a diner?"

"Let's go, gals," Nell called. She and Aggie pointed the teams to their rows.

There was a lot of talk as to how everyone had put one over on their menfolks. "This'll teach them to go out and play poker all night long," Tessie said.

From several rows over came the reply, "If he can stay out all night, I can."

As the night wore on, the women spread out across the fields, their lanterns looking like giant fireflies scattered throughout the darkness.

Nell took Alma's truck and left long enough to return to the house for food. In anticipation, Clara had risen and made stacks of sandwiches and coffee enough to fill all the pots they had. The containers were covered with lids, then put in the back of the truck. Nell threw a heavy blanket over them, hoping the blanket would keep the coffee from slopping too badly. In forty-five minutes she was back at the fields.

Aggie came over to the truck and helped herself to a sandwich and coffee. "I'll take a cup back with me. The rest'll smell it and be right over." She added, "Tessie's been doing a lot of singing tonight, Nell."

"She's pleased about the help."

"I think it's more than that."

Nell smiled. "Could be. I hope so." With a cup in each hand, she too headed back to work.

They harvested the first field by midnight. Working the second field a short distance away, they were quieter this time, the area bigger and the work seemingly heavier. The trucks were now filled, and the women were beginning to pack the cars, even the rumble seats.

At three, they loaded the final bag and returned to the house, their vehicles moving slowly under the burdensome weight of the potatoes.

"A hell of a crop," Nell kept saying over and over again. "A hell of a crop."

"Now all we have to do is get it to town," Aggie told her. The horses having long since been turned into the pasture, she asked, "Can we hitch our wagon to one of the trucks? I think we could get the rest to the depot that way."

"Any we can't we'll cram into the cars somehow," Alma promised.

At four a.m., the women trooped into the house.

They freshened up and ate again. Several pitched in, making more sandwiches.

"It's a good thing I baked bread yesterday," Clara said.

Nell watched the last slice disappear from the breadboard. She had hoped she would get a piece for herself. "Yeah, a good thing," she answered and looked at her watch. "Sun-up soon."

Every vehicle was now loaded to capacity. Passengers who had forfeited their seats for potatoes hopped onto running boards. At five a.m., eight trucks, seven cars and a wagon in tow started down the drive, headed for Grassy Flat's train depot.

It was slow going for the truck hauling the wagon, and those riding running boards became so chilled that by the time they had gone two miles, a halt was called so they could trade places with the drivers. They stopped three times, and just outside of town they gathered to talk, knowing that the men were on their way to the depot, too.

"What do you think they'll say when they see us?" Miranda asked.

"Doesn't matter now," Florence Gordon said. "What's done is done."

"We lied," Emily said.

"You knew that last night."

"So what do we do?"

"We'll know in five minutes," Nell answered.

CHAPTER NINETEEN

From the running board of Alma's truck where Aggie rode, she could see a long line of mule- and horse-drawn wagons and trucks already parked at the depot's loading platform. The men had spotted the caravan a half-mile from the town line and were drifting toward it, wondering, apparently, at the strange motorcade.

As the women drew nearer, gazes of curiosity quickly changed to questioning scowls, but the determined women did not stop until they pulled in behind the wagons. They jumped off the running boards and out of vehicles, immediately forming a protective group.

Harry Bibbs moved among the fellows, saying something to them.

"Look at that fat old toad," Alma said. "Already stirring them up."

Recognizing their kinfolk, the men approached the women.

Mort Bingham, a willowy fellow with a long, drooping mustache and bushy eyebrows, walked over to his vehicle and scrutinized its contents. Looking sharply at his wife, he asked, "What the hell do you think you're doing, Alma? Thought you said you was going to sit with Fred Houser's wife." He glanced at his truck. "And where'd you get these spuds?"

"They're Nell's and Aggie's," she answered. "And I changed my mind."

Having reached his own truck, William Beckwith asked, "What do you mean, Nell and Aggie's?" He pulled up the collar of his thick, sheepskin coat to ward off a cold gust. His hat brim flapped in the breeze.

Ramona hurried to his side. "Ain't it a dandy crop, William?"

Mort worked a wad of tobacco around his mouth, settling it in a cheek. "Not if it's in *my* truck, it ain't. Hey, boys," he yelled to those who had strung themselves out along the vehicles' line. "These look like your ve-hicles."

Angry shouts of acclamation were heard.

"Then the spuds are yours! Take 'em." He opened the door and reached for a sack.

"Like hell," Aggie shouted. She would have attacked Mort if Nell hadn't stopped her.

"You will not stoop to his level," Nell declared. "*I* will!" She spun on her heel and laid a resounding punch against his whiskered cheek.

Staggered by the unexpected blow, he reeled back a step or two, his eyes radiating hatred as he rubbed his face. "You little *whore.*"

"Nell, stop!" Alma barked. "Mort, you watch your mouth."

Nell stood toe to toe with him. "You try taking these potatoes, Beckwith, and I'll walk right over you."

"Now hold on here. What's going on?" Sheriff Bob Miner seemed to appear from nowhere, stepping between the adversaries.

Bibbs also came forward. "These women are operating illegally, Sheriff. I bet they ain't paid one red cent to rent these cars and trucks."

"Oh, shut up, Harry," Nell said. "I heard you're so full of sour grapes, you could be fermented for wine."

"Don't trust the sheriff," Aggie warned the women. "He's likely to stick with the boys if he thinks it'll get him votes."

"These bitches stole our trucks and our *wives!*" Mort bellowed.

"Nobody stole anything, Sheriff," Aggie protested. "Mort here says the potatoes are his since they're in his truck."

"We own the crop," Mort insisted, waving his arm toward his friends. His face had turned scarlet, the veins in his forehead visibly pulsing, his cud shifting rapidly from cheek to cheek. "Forced the womenfolk to come out and work and lie about it to their menfolk."

Nell protested furiously. "We did *not!*" Her arms flailed the air like windmills.

"My wife's been gone all night," a man shouted.

"Mine too," someone else said. "She's supposed to be helping Fred Houser's wife."

"Fred," came a call. "My old lady been over to your house last night?"

"Nope, nobody been there, 'cept Iva. Came to visit and never went home. Said she was having female problems and wanted EmmyLou to take care of her since her man didn't know what to do. Didn't look to me like she was having female problems."

Miner faced the irate men. "I don't give a damn what your wives do at night, boys. It ain't up to me to keep track of 'em. Now what I want to know is, who grew the spuds?"

Tessie marched forward announcing, "Nell and Aggie grew them."

Miner thoughtfully scratched the stubble on his chin. "The spuds are in your trucks, boys, and that might make them yours, but I doubt it. I'll go call the judge right now to check the law about ninety percent possession. And you folks calm down till I get back with an answer."

Before he had gone five yards, the women encircled him. They stood close to him, hemming him in. He backed up a step to free himself of them, but they stayed with him, moving forward, a silent ring of females ready to protect what was theirs, as though protecting their young.

Aggie's eyes were slits, her mouth drawn tight over her teeth. She stood the closest to him. "You're deliberately sitting on the fence, Miner, and law or no law, if you come back telling these men they can have my potatoes, you'll regret it."

"Every man will," Alma said. "We promise. I didn't bust my back digging all night just to give them away."

The others murmured sharp agreement.

His eyes scanned them. They had drawn to within inches of him, the circle tight now, tight enough to easily grab his gun. Someone put a hand on the butt, and he jumped. Looking across the tops of their heads, he said, "You can't take the spuds, boys, no matter whose ve-hicle they're in. It's a fact."

Daniel Hess's large black eyes flashed angrily. "You're not gonna call?"

"I'm not gonna call," Miner said. "No sense in it."

The hand fell from his gun, and the women let him through. He moved off to watch them, to let them decide their own end. The circle disintegrated, and the women started back to the motorcade.

A tall, lanky farmer stalked up to his wife. "Damn you, Edna Vogel, pull those potatoes outta my car, and get on back to the house. I'll see you later."

A second man ordered his wife home. Several followed his lead, telling their wives to dump the potatoes and go home, some badgering them, their faces only inches from their wives.

Mort grabbed Alma by the arm and pulled her aside. "You git too." Painfully, he slapped her bottom.

She twisted away from him. "You take your

hands off me Morton Bingham. I'm not a child to be spanked, *especially* in public, and I'm not moving until every spud in these cars and trucks are sold."

Daniel grabbed Lura. "No," she protested. "I leave when they're empty."

"Sit down, girls," Alma said, quickly dropping to the earth and madly patting it. "Sit down. They can't drag us through the street like dead horses." The women immediately flopped to the ground.

Mort roared at Alma, "*Get up,* or I'll haul your ass home!"

"Then do it! But Nell and Aggie are going to sell their potatoes. They've got just as much right to as you or anybody else."

Mort looked befuddled. "Why are you ladies *doing* this?"

"Because you men cut off their water," Miranda answered. "Led by Harry Bibbs. We're trying to make it right because *you* sure won't!"

His behind swinging like a running duck's, Bibbs hastened over to them roaring, "I got a right to fence!"

Mort backed him with gusto. "You bet you do, Harry! Tell 'em."

"Aggie and Nell got rights, too," Ramona retorted. "They got a right to water, and *I* got a right to help other women. Fact is, I got a right to come home *late* at night."

"Then who's gonna take care of the kids?" Fred Houser asked. "Who the hell's got them right now?"

"They're with those who couldn't help harvest," Alma answered. "They're well cared for."

"By damn!" Fred raged. He ripped off his hat and threw it on the ground. "Is that what I should expect when EmmyLou has our kid? For him to be farmed out while my wife goes gallivanting around all night."

"You gallivant all night," Ramona answered. "You men and your stupid all-night poker games!"

"You want to rethink your marriage?" Nell whispered to Emily.

"May have to," she whispered back.

Dusty, hearing the ruckus clear over to the Rock Wren, had shown up and was openly cursing the stupidity of the women.

"Oh, shut up, Dusty," Tessie snarled, still sitting in the road. "You helped fence, too. I heard you braggin' about it in the Rock Wren."

"Why you little loudmouth . . ." He reached for her. "*Come on*. It's time to go home."

She pulled away from him, saying, "I'm not going, Dusty."

"The hell you ain't. You've been buffaloed by these two girls." He looked toward Nell and Aggie sitting nearby. "Just like all the rest of them have."

Tessie shook her head. "No, Dusty, I haven't. I won't go with you, and I won't be home except to pick up my things. I'm finished with you."

Aggie's eyes grew big. "Tessie, don't be foolish." The other women began buzzing like bees.

"Just like that? You're leaving?" Dusty asked. "That's a laugh." He chuckled, but it sounded false as he glanced around at his friends who watched him closely.

Arrogantly, Tessie tossed back her head. "I was going to wait a day or two, but I have other plans, and they just won't keep."

Dusty's eyes looked like they had filled with molten fluid and were about to blow out of his head. "What a laugh! You never planned a thing in your life. I've made every decision you ever carried out."

"And that's exactly what's wrong here, this morning," Emily loudly pronounced. "I'm sick of having my decisions made for me. And don't you plan on making any for me either, Willie Thomas."

Amy Wetworth added "Come to think of it, the biggest decision I've made lately is what to wear to church."

"If Nell and Aggie can think for themselves, then so can I," announced Alice Smith.

Tim Smith bellowed a laugh. His big belly shook like a rumbling train. "That's hogwash, Alice. It wasn't but two nights ago you told me how sinful they were."

Alice defiantly folded her arms across her chest. "They get to make their own decisions."

"You sound just like a foolish little kid," he accused.

"Why, because I want to think for myself?"

"Let the women sit in the road, boys," Bibbs yelled. "Go get your trucks and grab their potatoes." The men immediately reacted to his suggestion.

Instantly, the women scrambled to their feet to overtake them.

Two shots rang out, splitting the air. "Hold on, damn it!" Sheriff Miner stepped into the hostile, milling crowd. "This has gone on long enough. From where I'm watching, this looks like pure foolishness. Now you men got a family squabble, no doubt about it. But those spuds belong to Nell Abbott and Aggie

Tucker. Let 'em sell them and be done with it. Then take your wives home and finish your fightin' there and not in the middle of town."

He didn't holster the .45 until Mort yelled over the heads of several people, "You'll not get another vote from me, Miner."

"Me neither," another man said.

A long whistle sounded in the distance. Men drifted, cursing, over to the loading platform. The women hung back, but remained nearby.

The train slowed to a stop, the steam from the engine hissing loudly. At the tail end of a long line of boxcars, Zed Trask jumped from the caboose and stepped onto the platform. He was a big, muscular man who for years had been handling the buying and selling of crops for companies in the east. "Got to make an announcement before we begin, gents," he told them. "I come up from south of here, and this train's already loaded with potatoes. Everybody's got a bumper crop this year. It's driven the price way down. The companies won't pay top dollar, but they'll buy all you have. So you can wait and try selling later, or you can sell right now and have money in your pockets today. I'm open for business." He turned his back on the furiously protesting sellers while he slid open an empty boxcar door and rolled out a heavy set of scales on wheels.

A big barrel-chested man shouldered his way through the group to the edge of the platform. "We're all broke, Zed. How the hell we supposed to get by on less than top dollar? The company men explain that?"

"I only know what they told me," he answered. "You can wait if you want to."

Outrage and anger filled the eyes of the growers, defeat quickly taking over. No one pulled out of line. They had been hungry too long. Tears of both men and women were excused as being caused by the winds that had turned sharply colder in the past half hour.

Dazed, Aggie asked, "Was all this for nothing?"

"I don't know," Nell answered, as stunned as Aggie.

The train would remain at the station for several days while farmers with animals and wagons made several trips before delivering their entire crop. Nell and Aggie and others with motor vehicles would complete delivery at once.

The prize potatoes they had worked so hard to raise in their vegetable garden and had dug up just before leaving this morning were beaten by a pound by Chester Olmstead. Aggie wanted to challenge the scales' honesty and shoot Chester dead where he stood. Nell was the cool-headed one.

"We planted and watered and harvested and sold our potatoes. We won. Against him. Against all of them. Be grateful."

"We didn't win," Aggie argued. "We barely broke even again." She read the check she had been handed earlier. It was fifty dollars more than last year.

The skies, so long without rain, had filled with thick gray clouds. Soon, a drizzle that could soak right through a body began to blanket the earth.

The women had emptied their vehicles. It was time for them to go. They gathered around Aggie and Nell.

"There's no way to thank you," Aggie said. "Just

no way. And you're probably all in a heap of trouble."

"Maybe," Miranda replied. "But Grassy Flats could do with a change or two. Anyway, glad to have been a help. It wasn't much."

"Digging potatoes all night is a great deal," Nell corrected. "And standing up to your husbands, to any man, is a great deal."

"We're all pretty damn good if you ask me," Emily replied.

Aggie felt her throat tighten. "Yes — you're all pretty damn good."

As the women drifted way, Emily asked Tessie, "You mean it about leaving Dusty?"

"I mean it," she replied firmly. "But don't leave Willie. He's a good man, and I think he learned a lot about you today."

Soon the area was cleared of all but the wagons slowly rolling to and from the depot, their drivers hunched against the changing weather.

Dusty, standing off to one side, still waited for his wife. "Come on, Tess, get in the car. We got customers waiting."

"You got customers waiting, Dusty. I told you I'm not going back."

"Stupid sow. You'll be back by supper." He stalked off, swearing and frequently glancing back at her.

"Only to get my things, Dusty. You'll have your car tomorrow morning."

He didn't argue, apparently still not believing her.

Aggie said, "You better know what you're doing, Tessie."

"Oh, he's so sure of himself," Tessie replied. "He thinks if he knocks me around the bedroom some, I'll behave like a well-trained cutting horse. I know what I'm doing, Aggie," she said with conviction.

"What are you doing?" Nell asked.

"I'll tell you on the way back to your farm. The answer's there."

As Tessie walked away, Aggie whispered to Nell, "Told you so."

"You sure did, Aggie, you sure did."

Sometimes, Aggie knew, Nell loved hearing "Told you so" from her.

CHAPTER TWENTY

Tessie and Clara walked into the kitchen. The table was littered with sheets of paper covered with figures. Nell was kneeling beside Aggie's chair, holding her tightly. Both women were crying. Tessie and Clara slipped quietly away.

Nell and Aggie had worked for hours, trying to stretch their dollars. There were not enough of them.

"It's not fair, Nell. It's just not fair. To have worked so hard, and for what?" In the end, their furniture, Nell's china and Aggie's piano and radio would have to wait. The truck would be all they could manage. When they ran out of money again, there would be very little left to sell.

Tears ran down both their faces, sobs racked their bodies.

"We'll be able to pay the mortgage for a while," Nell said, rocking Aggie back and forth. "That'll keep us safe. We have our home, Aggie. We didn't lose it. We didn't *lose* it."

Aggie pulled away from her and buried her face in her arms on the table. "But we will, Nell. We will. We'll run out of money again next summer, and Myers will be back nagging and nagging and nagging. I could *kill* that man." She slammed her fists over and over against the table until Nell grabbed them and crushed them against her chest.

"Stop," she whispered. "Stop. Aggie, honey, look at me. We'll think of something. We always do. Haven't we always? Haven't we?" She reached up and brushed away tears on Aggie's face.

"Oh God, Nell. I don't think I can stand it any longer."

Nell again drew her close. "We'll just try harder next year."

Aggie pulled away. Her eyes were red-rimmed, her lashes sticking together with copious tears. "Harder? How can you possibly try harder?"

Nell shrugged. "I don't know. I know I can, and I know I will, and I know you will too."

Aggie threw back her head. The words were wrenched from her soul. "Oh God, I know, I know." Her head fell against Nell's shoulder.

"We'll get your piano back, Aggie. If it's the last thing I ever do, I'll see you get the piano back."

"And you'll have your mother's china, Nell."

Nell's eyes flooded with pain. "If it's still in the pawn shop."

The following morning, the women, with Nettie riding comfortably in Clara's lap and Tessie driving, rode into Grassy Flats. They stopped at Mike Perry's. Dusty could pick up the car whenever he learned it was there.

They wandered out back of the shop to see if the Dodge was still around. Several vehicles were parked in one area and in another, a small corral held three horses. "More cars than horses," Tessie said. "Won't be long, you won't see horses anymore." She looked sadly at the animals nosing near the corral posts where thin tufts of brown grass still clung.

Aggie scanned the vehicles. "Good, the truck's still there." She studied its condition carefully. "Needs tires."

"Probably not all it needs," Nell said. "Let's go see if it's for sale."

"Everything Perry has is for sale," Tessie told them. "Even his wife."

"I've heard that," Aggie remarked.

They went in through the rear of the shop. "You here, Mike?" Nell called. She squinted, waiting for her eyes to adjust to the interior's dim light.

Perry crawled from beneath a car. He was covered with grease and oil. "Come sneakin' in the back door, Abbott?"

"I don't sneak," she retorted. "How much for my truck?"

He rose and wiped his hands on a rag. "Had to do a lot of work on it."

"Like what?" Aggie demanded. "Looks worse than when we sold it."

"Ain't." He walked to the door and looked out toward the Dodge. "Changed the oil, plugs, put on new tires."

"They're all bald," Nell answered.

"Ain't my fault. I don't know why they're bald. I put on new."

"How much?" Aggie asked.

"Hundred and ten."

Nell stormed over to him. "A hundred and ten! You only gave us fifty bucks for it."

"Times is better," Mike said. "Best I can do. Take it or leave it."

Nell and Aggie wandered off, leaving Tessie and Clara, with Nettie in her arms, to glare at Mike.

"We need the truck," Nell said.

"We could get something else."

"What? You saw what he has out there. The truck's the only decent-looking thing on the lot."

"We'll dicker."

They walked back to Mike. Tessie still scowled as though her face had permanently frozen into a demon's grimace.

"Give you seventy," Nell offered.

"Hundred and ten," Mike countered.

"Eighty."

"Hundred and ten."

"Eighty-five," Nell said, "and that's my final offer."

"Hundred and ten." He stuck his face into hers. "And that's *my* final offer."

From her pocket, Aggie whipped out a wad of bills that had been converted yesterday from check to cash. "Here, then, damn you. Take it!" With shaking hands, she counted out the money. Looking defiantly at him, she plunged it into a can of oil on a nearby bench.

"Hey," Mike yelled. "You can't do that." He took a threatening step toward her.

"Come on, girls," Nell said. "I've got the keys." She had snatched them from a keyboard attached to the wall. The women left him fishing through the oil and threatening them with a hanging if they ever came around again.

The others hopped inside while Nell, already behind the wheel, leaned on the starter. "Pray there's gas in this bucket of bolts," she said. It had obviously sat for a long time. The motor labored, then kicked into life. Like a well-directed chorus, the women collectively sighed with relief.

"Let's get your stuff, Tessie, and go home," Aggie said.

Later in the kitchen, Clara held Nettie in her lap, breast-feeding her. She looked around at each of the women seated at the table, her gaze long and studious.

"Clara, what on earth are you staring at?" Aggie asked.

"I was just thinking about the number of times we've sat here just like this, and planned the day.

What everyone would do, which fields would be planted or watered or hilled. Doesn't seem like six months since I came here.

"It doesn't," Aggie agreed. "A lot has happened."

"Same old stuff day after day," Nell said.

"Some of it wasn't," Aggie replied.

"Nope."

A car coming up the drive caught their attention. Jeff Myers shut off the engine and got out. He had no opportunity to even reach the porch steps before the women were out the door, blocking his way. Barney, standing beside Aggie, growled low, his back bristling.

"What do you want, Myers?" Aggie asked.

He drew a copy of their mortgage from a coat pocket. "Come to collect next month's mortgage payment."

Nell stepped off the porch and snatched it from his hand. "Why so early?"

"Saw you leave with your truck yesterday," he said. "You didn't have anything in the back — like your furniture. Something goes wrong, you have nothing left to sell. You should consider paying what money you have to keep the bank off you for as long as possible."

"And then what, Myers?" Nell asked. "Eat from our garden? 'Course the season's over. Or maybe we could eat our cow."

"And your chickens," he added. "You could do that, and the bank would be happy too."

"Happy?" Aggie said. "Happy?" Her voice had risen to a screech.

"You can do what you want, ladies," he said. "I'm just trying to make things easier for you."

"You're trying your best to take their farm, Jeff," Tessie said. Step by step, word by word, she approached him. "Do you think we're blind to you, to the men of this town, your scheming, conniving ways? Harassment, Jeff, that's all this is. Pure harassment."

"What about the rest of the farmers and ranchers?" Nell asked. "If you can, are you going to shut them down, too?"

"They aren't poor risks, Nell. They got families. Children to raise. They'll stick around."

Clara went inside and brought out Nettie. "We got a child, too, banker."

"What? Four women have a baby?" he laughed. "By the way, Tessie, Dusty told me to bring you back with me."

"Go to hell, Myers. I'm not going anywhere."

Myers studied the house. He turned and looked toward the barn and horses. "Don't think I'll have any trouble getting rid of the place."

"*AHHHHH!*" Like a rogue panther, Aggie flew off the porch, landing on the banker's back, driving him to the earth. With both fists, she pummeled his head and back. Using his ears as handles, she was smashing his face into the ground before Nell and Tessie could haul her off.

"That won't do us any good, Tucker," Nell yelled into her face.

Myers stood shakily and dusted off his coat and spat dirt from his mouth. He wiped blood from his nose, speaking in a trembling, hate-filled voice. "You'll be gone in a year, ladies. A year. I promise you that. And I'm going to have you arrested for assault and battery."

"It isn't my fault you fell off the porch," Aggie raged, jerking herself loose from Nell's clutches.

"That's right," Tessie agreed. "I saw the whole thing."

Clara propped Nettie in the rocking chair and picked up a potato fork leaning against the house. "Might be he busted his leg, too."

"He didn't," Tessie said, snatching the fork from her. "He only fell bad." She set the tool aside. "But he could break a leg if he comes here and falls off the porch again. You get my meaning, Myers?" she asked.

He backed away from the women and kept backing until he reached his car. Still facing them, he opened the door. Inside, he adjusted his rearview mirror, keeping them in his sights. The engine started, and he was gone.

That evening Nell found Clara sitting alone in the kitchen. The others had gone to bed. A lamp burned low on the table.

Nell joined her. "You all right?"

She sighed. "Next to you and Aggie, I'm doing great. You're so close to losing everything you own, I don't know how you manage not to let it do awful things to you."

"Like what?"

"Like fight with Aggie until you can't stand the sight of each other, like hate life to the point of wanting to quit. It did that to me when Hank left."

Nell tipped back in the chair. "I don't know, Clara. We'll make out. Somehow, we always do. I'm getting awful sick of saying that, though. Maybe we'll just give up the ghost and go on back to Boise."

"How long you two been together?" Clara asked.

"Going on sixteen years."

"Ever wonder if you made a mistake?"

Nell smiled. "No, just wondered from time to time how I came to be so lucky to have found Aggie."

"And we're just starting out, me and Tess and Nettie."

"You'll be fine."

"How'll we get over the tough times? You and Aggie yell and scream at each other, and it doesn't seem to hurt you."

"Oh, it hurts, but no marriage is all romance. There's dry spells and wet spells and times when it feels like a great vacuum has taken us over and it'd be better to be alone than to deal with one more problem between us."

"But you've always survived."

"You worried about you and Tessie?"

"Some."

"It's going to be better than with Hank."

"Why should it?"

"Because Tess is a woman, and women understand each other better than men understand women."

Idly, Clara traced the pattern on the tablecloth. "All I know is that you and Aggie have been through hell, and you still seem closer than ever. I want that. I want that nothing can ever drive me and Tess apart."

"You have to work at it. It doesn't come easy."

"I've seen that."

"But it does come."

Clara nodded. "Might be me and Tessie could help you one day."

Nell smiled. "You already have. Why don't you go on up to her now. She's waiting, I bet."

Clara blushed mightily. "I'll go up soon."

Nell patted her shoulder and left her.

Clara shook her head, amazed that she had ever loved Hank. He had always thought only of himself. She'd always known that about him, but she took it as a part of marriage, thinking that was how it was supposed to be. Tess didn't seem to be like that at all.

"If you and Aggie can do it, Nell," she said into the darkness, "then Tessie and Nettie and I can."

She went upstairs to tell Tessie so.

A few of the publications of
THE NAIAD PRESS, INC.
P.O. Box 10543 • Tallahassee, Florida 32302
Phone (904) 539-5965
Mail orders welcome. Please include 15% postage.

A CERTAIN DISCONTENT by Cleve Boutell. 240 pp. A unique
coterie of women.   ISBN 1-56280-009-4 $9.95

GRASSY FLATS by Penny Hayes. 256 pp. Lesbian romance in
the '30s.   ISBN 1-56280-010-8   9.95

A SINGULAR SPY by Amanda K. Williams. 192 pp. 3rd spy novel
featuring Lesbian agent Madison McGuire.   ISBN 1-56280-008-6   8.95

THE END OF APRIL by Penny Sumner. 240 pp. A Victoria Cross
Mystery. First in a series.   ISBN 1-56280-007-8   8.95

A FLIGHT OF ANGELS by Sarah Aldridge. 240 pp. Romance set at
the National Gallery of Art   ISBN 1-56280-001-9   9.95

HOUSTON TOWN by Deborah Powell. 208 pp. A Hollis Carpenter
mystery. Second in a series.   ISBN 1-56280-006-X   8.95

KISS AND TELL by Robbi Sommers. 192 pp. Scorching stories by
the author of *Pleasures*.   ISBN 1-56280-005-1   8.95

STILL WATERS by Pat Welch. 208 pp. Second in the Helen
Black mystery series.   ISBN 0-941483-97-5   8.95

MURDER IS GERMANE by Karen Saum. 224 pp. The 2nd
Brigid Donovan mystery.   ISBN 0-941483-98-3   8.95

TO LOVE AGAIN by Evelyn Kennedy. 208 pp. Wildly
romantic love story.   ISBN 0-941483-85-1   9.95

IN THE GAME by Nikki Baker. 192 pp. A Virginia Kelly
mystery. First in a series.   ISBN 01-56280-004-3   8.95

AVALON by Mary Jane Jones. 256 pp. A Lesbian Arthurian
romance.   ISBN 0-941483-96-7   9.95

STRANDED by Camarin Grae. 320 pp. Entertaining, riveting
adventure.   ISBN 0-941483-99-1   9.95

THE DAUGHTERS OF ARTEMIS by Lauren Wright Douglas.
240 pp. Third Caitlin Reece mystery.   ISBN 0-941483-95-9   8.95

CLEARWATER by Catherine Ennis. 176 pp. Romantic secrets
of a small Louisiana town.   ISBN 0-941483-65-7   8.95

THE HALLELUJAH MURDERS by Dorothy Tell. 176 pp.
Second Poppy Dillworth mystery.   ISBN 0-941483-88-6   8.95

ZETA BASE by Judith Alguire. 208 pp. Lesbian triangle
on a future Earth.   ISBN 0-941483-94-0   9.95

SECOND CHANCE by Jackie Calhoun. 256 pp. Contemporary
Lesbian lives and loves.   ISBN 0-941483-93-2   9.95

MURDER BY TRADITION by Katherine V. Forrest. 288 pp.
A Kate Delafield Mystery. 4th in a series.   ISBN 0-941483-89-4   18.95

BENEDICTION by Diane Salvatore. 272 pp. Striking,
contemporary romantic novel.   ISBN 0-941483-90-8   9.95

CALLING RAIN by Karen Marie Christa Minns. 240 pp.
Spellbinding, erotic love story   ISBN 0-941483-87-8   9.95

BLACK IRIS by Jeane Harris. 192 pp. Caroline's hidden past . . .
                                        ISBN 0-941483-68-1   8.95

TOUCHWOOD by Karin Kallmaker. 240 pp. Loving, May/
December romance.   ISBN 0-941483-76-2   8.95

BAYOU CITY SECRETS by Deborah Powell. 224 pp. A Hollis
Carpenter mystery. First in a series.   ISBN 0-941483-91-6   8.95

COP OUT by Claire McNab. 208 pp. 4th Det. Insp. Carol Ashton
mystery.   ISBN 0-941483-84-3   8.95

LODESTAR by Phyllis Horn. 224 pp. Romantic, fast-moving
adventure.   ISBN 0-941483-83-5   8.95

THE BEVERLY MALIBU by Katherine V. Forrest. 288 pp. A
Kate Delafield Mystery. 3rd in a series. (HC)   ISBN 0-941483-47-9   16.95
                            Paperback   ISBN 0-941483-48-7   9.95

THAT OLD STUDEBAKER by Lee Lynch. 272 pp. Andy's affair
with Regina and her attachment to her beloved car.
                                        ISBN 0-941483-82-7   9.95

PASSION'S LEGACY by Lori Paige. 224 pp. Sarah is swept into
the arms of Augusta Pym in this delightful historical romance.
                                        ISBN 0-941483-81-9   8.95

THE PROVIDENCE FILE by Amanda Kyle Williams. 256 pp.
Second espionage thriller featuring lesbian agent Madison McGuire
                                        ISBN 0-941483-92-4   8.95

I LEFT MY HEART by Jaye Maiman. 320 pp. A Robin Miller
Mystery. First in a series.   ISBN 0-941483-72-X   9.95

THE PRICE OF SALT by Patricia Highsmith (writing as Claire
Morgan). 288 pp. Classic lesbian novel, first issued in 1952 . . .
acknowledged by its author under her own, very famous, name.
                                        ISBN 1-56280-003-5   8.95

SIDE BY SIDE by Isabel Miller. 256 pp. From beloved author of
Patience and Sarah.   ISBN 0-941483-77-0   8.95

SOUTHBOUND by Sheila Ortiz Taylor. 240 pp. Hilarious sequel
to *Faultline*.   ISBN 0-941483-78-9   8.95

STAYING POWER: LONG TERM LESBIAN COUPLES
by Susan E. Johnson. 352 pp. Joys of coupledom.
                                        ISBN 0-941-483-75-4   12.95

SLICK by Camarin Grae. 304 pp. Exotic, erotic adventure.
                                    ISBN 0-941483-74-6   9.95
NINTH LIFE by Lauren Wright Douglas. 256 pp. A Caitlin
Reece mystery. 2nd in a series.   ISBN 0-941483-50-9   8.95
PLAYERS by Robbi Sommers. 192 pp. Sizzling, erotic novel.
                                    ISBN 0-941483-73-8   8.95
MURDER AT RED ROOK RANCH by Dorothy Tell. 224 pp.
First Poppy Dillworth adventure.   ISBN 0-941483-80-0   8.95
LESBIAN SURVIVAL MANUAL by Rhonda Dicksion.
112 pp. Cartoons!   ISBN 0-941483-71-1   8.95
A ROOM FULL OF WOMEN by Elisabeth Nonas. 256 pp.
Contemporary Lesbian lives.   ISBN 0-941483-69-X   8.95
MURDER IS RELATIVE by Karen Saum. 256 pp. The first
Brigid Donovan mystery.   ISBN 0-941483-70-3   8.95
PRIORITIES by Lynda Lyons 288 pp. Science fiction with
a twist.   ISBN 0-941483-66-5   8.95
THEME FOR DIVERSE INSTRUMENTS by Jane Rule. 208
pp. Powerful romantic lesbian stories. ISBN 0-941483-63-0   8.95
LESBIAN QUERIES by Hertz & Ertman. 112 pp. The questions
you were too embarrassed to ask.   ISBN 0-941483-67-3   8.95
CLUB 12 by Amanda Kyle Williams. 288 pp. Espionage thriller
featuring a lesbian agent!   ISBN 0-941483-64-9   8.95
DEATH DOWN UNDER by Claire McNab. 240 pp. 3rd Det.
Insp. Carol Ashton mystery.   ISBN 0-941483-39-8   8.95
MONTANA FEATHERS by Penny Hayes. 256 pp. Vivian and
Elizabeth find love in frontier Montana. ISBN 0-941483-61-4   8.95
CHESAPEAKE PROJECT by Phyllis Horn. 304 pp. Jessie &
Meredith in perilous adventure.   ISBN 0-941483-58-4   8.95
LIFESTYLES by Jackie Calhoun. 224 pp. Contemporary Lesbian
lives and loves.   ISBN 0-941483-57-6   8.95
VIRAGO by Karen Marie Christa Minns. 208 pp. Darsen has
chosen Ginny.   ISBN 0-941483-56-8   8.95
WILDERNESS TREK by Dorothy Tell. 192 pp. Six women on
vacation learning "new" skills.   ISBN 0-941483-60-6   8.95
MURDER BY THE BOOK by Pat Welch. 256 pp. A Helen
Black Mystery. First in a series.   ISBN 0-941483-59-2   8.95
BERRIGAN by Vicki P. McConnell. 176 pp. Youthful Lesbian —
romantic, idealistic Berrigan.   ISBN 0-941483-55-X   8.95
LESBIANS IN GERMANY by Lillian Faderman & B. Eriksson.
128 pp. Fiction, poetry, essays.   ISBN 0-941483-62-2   8.95

THERE'S SOMETHING I'VE BEEN MEANING TO TELL
YOU Ed. by Loralee MacPike. 288 pp. Gay men and lesbians
coming out to their children.   ISBN 0-941483-44-4   9.95
                                       ISBN 0-941483-54-1   16.95

LIFTING BELLY by Gertrude Stein. Ed. by Rebecca Mark. 104
pp. Erotic poetry.   ISBN 0-941483-51-7   8.95
                                       ISBN 0-941483-53-3   14.95

ROSE PENSKI by Roz Perry. 192 pp. Adult lovers in a long-term
relationship.   ISBN 0-941483-37-1   8.95

AFTER THE FIRE by Jane Rule. 256 pp. Warm, human novel
by this incomparable author.   ISBN 0-941483-45-2   8.95

SUE SLATE, PRIVATE EYE by Lee Lynch. 176 pp. The gay
folk of Peacock Alley are *all cats*.   ISBN 0-941483-52-5   8.95

CHRIS by Randy Salem. 224 pp. Golden oldie. Handsome Chris
and her adventures.   ISBN 0-941483-42-8   8.95

THREE WOMEN by March Hastings. 232 pp. Golden oldie. A
triangle among wealthy sophisticates.   ISBN 0-941483-43-6   8.95

RICE AND BEANS by Valeria Taylor. 232 pp. Love and
romance on poverty row.   ISBN 0-941483-41-X   8.95

PLEASURES by Robbi Sommers. 204 pp. Unprecedented
eroticism.   ISBN 0-941483-49-5   8.95

EDGEWISE by Camarin Grae. 372 pp. Spellbinding
adventure.   ISBN 0-941483-19-3   9.95

FATAL REUNION by Claire McNab. 224 pp. 2nd Det. Inspec.
Carol Ashton mystery.   ISBN 0-941483-40-1   8.95

KEEP TO ME STRANGER by Sarah Aldridge. 372 pp. Romance
set in a department store dynasty.   ISBN 0-941483-38-X   9.95

HEARTSCAPE by Sue Gambill. 204 pp. American lesbian in
Portugal.   ISBN 0-941483-33-9   8.95

IN THE BLOOD by Lauren Wright Douglas. 252 pp. Lesbian
science fiction adventure fantasy   ISBN 0-941483-22-3   8.95

THE BEE'S KISS by Shirley Verel. 216 pp. Delicate, delicious
romance.   ISBN 0-941483-36-3   8.95

RAGING MOTHER MOUNTAIN by Pat Emmerson. 264 pp.
Furosa Firechild's adventures in Wonderland.   ISBN 0-941483-35-5   8.95

IN EVERY PORT by Karin Kallmaker. 228 pp. Jessica's sexy,
adventuresome travels.   ISBN 0-941483-37-7   8.95

OF LOVE AND GLORY by Evelyn Kennedy. 192 pp. Exciting
WWII romance.   ISBN 0-941483-32-0   8.95

CLICKING STONES by Nancy Tyler Glenn. 288 pp. Love
transcending time.   ISBN 0-941483-31-2   9.95

SURVIVING SISTERS by Gail Pass. 252 pp. Powerful love
story.   ISBN 0-941483-16-9   8.95

SOUTH OF THE LINE by Catherine Ennis. 216 pp. Civil War
adventure.   ISBN 0-941483-29-0   8.95

WOMAN PLUS WOMAN by Dolores Klaich. 300 pp. Supurb
Lesbian overview.   ISBN 0-941483-28-2   9.95

SLOW DANCING AT MISS POLLY'S by Sheila Ortiz Taylor.
96 pp. Lesbian Poetry   ISBN 0-941483-30-4   7.95

DOUBLE DAUGHTER by Vicki P. McConnell. 216 pp. A Nyla
Wade Mystery, third in the series.   ISBN 0-941483-26-6   8.95

HEAVY GILT by Delores Klaich. 192 pp. Lesbian detective/
disappearing homophobes/upper class gay society.
                                          ISBN 0-941483-25-8   8.95

THE FINER GRAIN by Denise Ohio. 216 pp. Brilliant young
college lesbian novel.   ISBN 0-941483-11-8   8.95

THE AMAZON TRAIL by Lee Lynch. 216 pp. Life, travel & lore
of famous lesbian author.   ISBN 0-941483-27-4   8.95

HIGH CONTRAST by Jessie Lattimore. 264 pp. Women of the
Crystal Palace.   ISBN 0-941483-17-7   8.95

OCTOBER OBSESSION by Meredith More. Josie's rich, secret
Lesbian life.   ISBN 0-941483-18-5   8.95

LESBIAN CROSSROADS by Ruth Baetz. 276 pp. Contemporary
Lesbian lives.   ISBN 0-941483-21-5   9.95

BEFORE STONEWALL: THE MAKING OF A GAY AND
LESBIAN COMMUNITY by Andrea Weiss & Greta Schiller.
96 pp., 25 illus.   ISBN 0-941483-20-7   7.95

WE WALK THE BACK OF THE TIGER by Patricia A. Murphy.
192 pp. Romantic Lesbian novel/beginning women's movement.
                                          ISBN 0-941483-13-4   8.95

SUNDAY'S CHILD by Joyce Bright. 216 pp. Lesbian athletics, at
last the novel about sports.   ISBN 0-941483-12-6   8.95

OSTEN'S BAY by Zenobia N. Vole. 204 pp. Sizzling adventure
romance set on Bonaire.   ISBN 0-941483-15-0   8.95

LESSONS IN MURDER by Claire McNab. 216 pp. 1st Det. Inspec.
Carol Ashton mystery — erotic tension!.   ISBN 0-941483-14-2   8.95

YELLOWTHROAT by Penny Hayes. 240 pp. Margarita, bandit,
kidnaps Julia.   ISBN 0-941483-10-X   8.95

SAPPHISTRY: THE BOOK OF LESBIAN SEXUALITY by
Pat Califia. 3d edition, revised. 208 pp. ISBN 0-941483-24-X   8.95

CHERISHED LOVE by Evelyn Kennedy. 192 pp. Erotic
Lesbian love story.   ISBN 0-941483-08-8   8.95

LAST SEPTEMBER by Helen R. Hull. 208 pp. Six stories & a
glorious novella.   ISBN 0-941483-09-6   8.95

THE SECRET IN THE BIRD by Camarin Grae. 312 pp. Striking,
psychological suspense novel.   ISBN 0-941483-05-3   8.95

TO THE LIGHTNING by Catherine Ennis. 208 pp. Romantic
Lesbian 'Robinson Crusoe' adventure.   ISBN 0-941483-06-1   8.95

THE OTHER SIDE OF VENUS by Shirley Verel. 224 pp.
Luminous, romantic love story.   ISBN 0-941483-07-X   8.95

DREAMS AND SWORDS by Katherine V. Forrest. 192 pp.
Romantic, erotic, imaginative stories.   ISBN 0-941483-03-7   8.95

MEMORY BOARD by Jane Rule. 336 pp. Memorable novel
about an aging Lesbian couple.   ISBN 0-941483-02-9   9.95

THE ALWAYS ANONYMOUS BEAST by Lauren Wright
Douglas. 224 pp. A Caitlin Reece mystery. First in a series.
                                               ISBN 0-941483-04-5   8.95

SEARCHING FOR SPRING by Patricia A. Murphy. 224 pp.
Novel about the recovery of love.   ISBN 0-941483-00-2   8.95

DUSTY'S QUEEN OF HEARTS DINER by Lee Lynch. 240 pp.
Romantic blue-collar novel.   ISBN 0-941483-01-0   8.95

PARENTS MATTER by Ann Muller. 240 pp. Parents'
relationships with Lesbian daughters and gay sons.
                                               ISBN 0-930044-91-6   9.95

THE PEARLS by Shelley Smith. 176 pp. Passion and fun in
the Caribbean sun.   ISBN 0-930044-93-2   7.95

MAGDALENA by Sarah Aldridge. 352 pp. Epic Lesbian novel
set on three continents.   ISBN 0-930044-99-1   8.95

THE BLACK AND WHITE OF IT by Ann Allen Shockley.
144 pp. Short stories.   ISBN 0-930044-96-7   7.95

SAY JESUS AND COME TO ME by Ann Allen Shockley. 288
pp. Contemporary romance.   ISBN 0-930044-98-3   8.95

LOVING HER by Ann Allen Shockley. 192 pp. Romantic love
story.   ISBN 0-930044-97-5   7.95

MURDER AT THE NIGHTWOOD BAR by Katherine V.
Forrest. 240 pp. A Kate Delafield mystery. Second in a series.
                                               ISBN 0-930044-92-4   9.95

ZOE'S BOOK by Gail Pass. 224 pp. Passionate, obsessive love
story.   ISBN 0-930044-95-9   7.95

WINGED DANCER by Camarin Grae. 228 pp. Erotic Lesbian
adventure story.   ISBN 0-930044-88-6   8.95

PAZ by Camarin Grae. 336 pp. Romantic Lesbian adventurer
with the power to change the world.   ISBN 0-930044-89-4   8.95

SOUL SNATCHER by Camarin Grae. 224 pp. A puzzle, an
adventure, a mystery — Lesbian romance.   ISBN 0-930044-90-8   8.95

THE LOVE OF GOOD WOMEN by Isabel Miller. 224 pp.
Long-awaited new novel by the author of the beloved *Patience
and Sarah.*   ISBN 0-930044-81-9   8.95

THE HOUSE AT PELHAM FALLS by Brenda Weathers. 240
pp. Suspenseful Lesbian ghost story.   ISBN 0-930044-79-7   7.95

HOME IN YOUR HANDS by Lee Lynch. 240 pp. More stories
from the author of *Old Dyke Tales.*   ISBN 0-930044-80-0   7.95

EACH HAND A MAP by Anita Skeen. 112 pp. Real-life poems
that touch us all.   ISBN 0-930044-82-7   6.95

SURPLUS by Sylvia Stevenson. 342 pp. A classic early Lesbian
novel.   ISBN 0-930044-78-9   7.95

PEMBROKE PARK by Michelle Martin. 256 pp. Derring-do
and daring romance in Regency England.   ISBN 0-930044-77-0   7.95

THE LONG TRAIL by Penny Hayes. 248 pp. Vivid adventures
of two women in love in the old west.   ISBN 0-930044-76-2   8.95

HORIZON OF THE HEART by Shelley Smith. 192 pp. Hot
romance in summertime New England.   ISBN 0-930044-75-4   7.95

AN EMERGENCE OF GREEN by Katherine V. Forrest. 288
pp. Powerful novel of sexual discovery.   ISBN 0-930044-69-X   9.95

THE LESBIAN PERIODICALS INDEX edited by Claire
Potter. 432 pp. Author & subject index.   ISBN 0-930044-74-6   29.95

DESERT OF THE HEART by Jane Rule. 224 pp. A classic;
basis for the movie *Desert Hearts.*   ISBN 0-930044-73-8   8.95

SPRING FORWARD/FALL BACK by Sheila Ortiz Taylor.
288 pp. Literary novel of timeless love.   ISBN 0-930044-70-3   7.95

FOR KEEPS by Elisabeth Nonas. 144 pp. Contemporary novel
about losing and finding love.   ISBN 0-930044-71-1   7.95

TORCHLIGHT TO VALHALLA by Gale Wilhelm. 128 pp.
Classic novel by a great Lesbian writer.   ISBN 0-930044-68-1   7.95

LESBIAN NUNS: BREAKING SILENCE edited by Rosemary
Curb and Nancy Manahan. 432 pp. Unprecedented autobiographies
of religious life.   ISBN 0-930044-62-2   9.95

THE SWASHBUCKLER by Lee Lynch. 288 pp. Colorful novel
set in Greenwich Village in the sixties.   ISBN 0-930044-66-5   8.95

MISFORTUNE'S FRIEND by Sarah Aldridge. 320 pp. Histori-
cal Lesbian novel set on two continents.   ISBN 0-930044-67-3   7.95

A STUDIO OF ONE'S OWN by Ann Stokes. Edited by
Dolores Klaich. 128 pp. Autobiography.   ISBN 0-930044-64-9   7.95

SEX VARIANT WOMEN IN LITERATURE by Jeannette
Howard Foster. 448 pp. Literary history.   ISBN 0-930044-65-7   8.95

ANNA'S COUNTRY by Elizabeth Lang. 208 pp. A woman
finds her Lesbian identity.   ISBN 0-930044-19-3   8.95

PRISM by Valerie Taylor. 158 pp. A love affair between two
women in their sixties.   ISBN 0-930044-18-5   6.95

THE MARQUISE AND THE NOVICE by Victoria Ramstetter.
108 pp. A Lesbian Gothic novel.   ISBN 0-930044-16-9   6.95

OUTLANDER by Jane Rule. 207 pp. Short stories and essays
by one of our finest writers.   ISBN 0-930044-17-7   8.95

ALL TRUE LOVERS by Sarah Aldridge. 292 pp. Romantic
novel set in the 1930s and 1940s.   ISBN 0-930044-10-X   8.95

A WOMAN APPEARED TO ME by Renee Vivien. 65 pp. A
classic; translated by Jeannette H. Foster.   ISBN 0-930044-06-1   5.00

CYTHEREA'S BREATH by Sarah Aldridge. 240 pp. Romantic
novel about women's entrance into medicine.
                                                ISBN 0-930044-02-9   6.95

TOTTIE by Sarah Aldridge. 181 pp. Lesbian romance in the
turmoil of the sixties.   ISBN 0-930044-01-0   6.95

THE LATECOMER by Sarah Aldridge. 107 pp. A delicate love
story.   ISBN 0-930044-00-2   6.95

ODD GIRL OUT by Ann Bannon.   ISBN 0-930044-83-5   5.95
I AM A WOMAN 84-3; WOMEN IN THE SHADOWS 85-1;   each
JOURNEY TO A WOMAN 86-X; BEEBO BRINKER 87-8. Golden
oldies about life in Greenwich Village.

JOURNEY TO FULFILLMENT, A WORLD WITHOUT MEN, and   3.95
RETURN TO LESBOS. All by Valerie Taylor   each

These are just a few of the many Naiad Press titles — we are the oldest and
largest lesbian/feminist publishing company in the world. Please request a
complete catalog. We offer personal service; we encourage and welcome direct
mail orders from individuals who have limited access to bookstores carrying
our publications.